FOUR LOVE

EVER AND ALWAYS DUET, BOOK 2

JAYNE RYLON

HAPPY ENDINGS PUBLISHING

V2

eBook ISBN: 978-1-947093-15-7

Print ISBN: 978-1-947093-16-4

Cover Design by Jayne Rylon

Editing by Mackenzie Walton

Proofreading by Fedora Chen

Formatting by Jayne Rylon

ABOUT THE BOOK

The Ever & Always Duet concludes with Four Love...

Holly has never been more scared in her life. She's hoping that the bad guys attempting to bank off her realize—like she has—that her temporary husband doesn't care for her as anything more than a way to cash in on his inheritance and amuse his roommates in the process.

Even if she makes it out alive, she won't ever be whole. Not unless Trent, Lorenzo, and Owen suddenly decide that the stakes in the game they were playing are a lot steeper than can be paid for with money.

This time, they're gambling everything on love.

Four Love is the conclusion of the Ever & Always Duet, and should be read following Four Money.

ADDITIONAL INFORMATION

Sign up for the Naughty News for contests, release updates, news, appearance information, sneak peek excerpts, reading-themed apparel deals, and more. www.jaynerylon.com/newsletter

Shop for autographed books, reading-themed apparel, goodies, and more www.jaynerylon.com/shop

A complete list of Jayne's books can be found at www.jaynerylon.com/books

1

<hr>

Trent stared at the red numbers glowing on his clock. Six a.m. He'd lain there, awake, since his wife, Holly, had stormed out of his bedroom—his home, and maybe his life, too—just before midnight. The only thing that had made it worse was the fight he'd had with his two best friends following her departure.

Rare anger had marred Lorenzo's face as he'd lit into Trent, not only for fucking up the incredible foursome he, Owen, and Trent had just finished having with Holly, but also because he was pissed that Trent had scared her away entirely.

Reliving his mistakes and the hurt he'd caused the three people he gave a shit about most in the world had kept Trent wired all night. He might as well get up. Visiting hours at the hospital where Holly's mother was recovering from a kidney transplant started soon, and he intended to be there in case Holly needed him. Hell, he was hoping she would tolerate him nearby and that she wouldn't send him away like his own family had while his father lay dying in the same building.

He wouldn't blame her if she did, though.

Trent rolled out of bed, accepting the single open-eyed glare from his dog Moose—who seemed just as irritated with him as everyone else because Holly wasn't there to pet him—and then trudged into kitchen to make a pitcher of extra-strong coffee.

He froze when he realized both Lorenzo and Owen were already sitting at the table, dressed, huddled over their own steaming cups as if they hadn't slept a wink more than he had.

Should he turn around? They had made it perfectly clear they didn't want to be near him if he was going to continue being a colossal fuck-up.

"Guys..." His throat threatened to slam shut, as if he were allergic to apologizing or eating humble pie.

"Nah, don't say it." Lorenzo waved him off. "You're an idiot, yes, but I get why last night was a recipe for disaster."

"You do?" Trent wished the guy would fill him in because nothing was making sense. One minute he had been having the best night of his life, and the next... It had fallen apart, exactly as he'd feared.

"We do." Owen nodded. He picked up the pot of coffee and poured some into the third mug on the table, the one they'd set out for him. "It's because you care about her. A lot. And it's scaring the shit out of you. She was getting too close, so you shoved her away."

Trent had come to the same conclusion sometime around three in the morning, so he didn't bother to deny it, instead kicking the chair out from the table and sinking into it. Even though his coffee scalded his mouth, he downed a few gulps of his drink. Sometimes what you needed most had the power to burn you.

Holly was no exception.

Trent put his face in his hand and scrubbed his bleary eyes. "So how do I fix this?"

"We're going to the hospital together. First, we'll make sure Holly and her mom are okay. Then we're going to beg her to give you—*us*—another chance and explain how your family refusing to accept you makes you think no one will, not even a woman as open-minded and perfect for us as Holly." Owen bobbed his head to punctuate each step as if he was speaking to a child.

Trent deserved that.

And even though he knew that was probably what they should do, some part of him still recoiled like a bug caught in bright light, scurrying away from the thing it was most afraid of.

"What if she doesn't want to come back?" Trent whispered before fortifying himself with several more long glugs of coffee.

"We'll have to figure that out on the fly." Lorenzo knocked his knee into Trent's. "But I honestly don't think that's going to be the case. I saw her last night. The way she looked at you. It wasn't only about sex. If she knows you care for her too, maybe she won't keep running. I *hope* she won't."

Trent winced, realizing what it must have done to Lorenzo to be walked out on with his pants down by the first woman he was getting attached to since he'd been left at the altar. Had to suck. And Trent had caused it. For the first time, he realized how much his roommates were banking on him, and he didn't want to let them down.

"Now go get dressed. Wear the blue shirt Lorenzo bought you for Christmas." Owen pointed toward the bedroom Trent had barely emerged from.

He grumbled but rose, draining the last of his cup before clunking it onto the table, resigned. "Fine. But you two are coming with me, right?"

"We wouldn't risk letting you screw this up for all of us. Again." Lorenzo was mostly giving him shit, his mouth quirked up in one corner. But there was a kernel of truth to his ribbing.

That was fine with Trent. He felt better with them by his side. Though the three of them were damaged in some way, together they balanced each other out. All of them might have a shot at convincing Holly they were worth a second chance.

~

TRENT GRIPPED the rail on the elevator wall hard enough he was afraid he might put a dent in the thing. He hadn't felt as much ominous dread in the pit of his stomach when he'd been waiting to hear about his father's prognosis.

Holly's reaction felt like a matter of life or death.

His happiness—as well as his best friends'—was hanging in the balance.

"It's going to be okay," Owen promised.

"She's going to forgive you, as long as you're honest with her," Lorenzo agreed. "You can't hold anything back. It's risky, yeah, but you have to put it all out there."

"So I should admit that I'm falling for her. Hard? You're sure?"

Both of his friends looked at him like he was stupid and said, "Yes!"

"Some groveling might not be bad either." Owen smacked him in the gut. "You hurt her, asshole. I saw the pain in her eyes when you offered to pay her to stick around and entertain us in bed for a few more months."

"I didn't—"

"Whether or not that's how you meant it, that's how she took your suggestion." Lorenzo shrugged. "You need to tell her your relationship isn't about the cash or your business anymore. This is something more."

Had it ever really been about the money? Sure, marrying Holly "temporarily" had satisfied the clause of his trust and allowed him to inherit an obscene amount of cash. It had made it possible for her mom to get the transplant she needed and paved the way for all his dreams—starting his own company *and* meeting someone who could desire the same type of relationship he did—to come true.

Suddenly, that was all that mattered. He couldn't wreck the chance to show her that no matter how desperately he'd craved success, she was what he needed. He wanted to give her everything he had, and for a hell of a lot longer than ninety days.

"*So* much more." Trent banged his head against the rear wall of the car as they glided to a stop on the floor housing the ICU. "But mostly, I have to make sure she's okay."

He couldn't stand the thought of her alone and afraid for her mother in addition to stressing about what had happened between them the night before.

Lorenzo smirked. "See?"

"What?" Trent tipped his head to the side like Moose sometimes did when he couldn't comprehend what his owner was doing.

"You care." Owen crossed his arms as they exited the elevator together.

"I do. Even if I should know better." Trent groaned. That had never worked out for him before.

Then he put his own shit on the back burner as he approached Holly's mom's room. The door hung open. The early morning glow of the desert surrounding them illuminated her private space. He peeked in at Mrs. Hendricks, who appeared to be sleeping.

No sign of Holly. Damn it! Had she gone to the cafeteria to grab breakfast?

"You can go in. She's been awake on and off." One of the nurses passing by shooed them inside, out of the way.

"Mrs. Hendricks?" Trent called softly, feeling awkward as hell intruding on the recovering woman without her daughter present.

The woman took several tries to blink her eyes open. Then she smiled. "Hey. Where's Holly?"

"She hasn't been here yet this morning?" Trent couldn't believe that. Mrs. Hendricks must mean Holly had stepped outside or gone to run a quick errand.

Without an ounce of doubt or confusion, Mrs. Hendricks shook her head slightly. "No. Haven't seen her since they rolled me into the operating room."

Trent's stomach dropped. Surely Mrs. Hendricks had simply forgotten about her daughter's presence since she had been so recently under sedation and was on some heavy-duty pain medication as well. That had to be the case. Didn't it?

"She... Well, shit, I don't exactly know where she is." Trent squashed the unease bubbling within him before it could boil into full blown panic.

Lorenzo elbowed him when Mrs. Hendricks tried to sit up, and failed. The monitor beside her bed showed her blood pressure spiking.

"Sorry. Let me go find out." Trent tried to smile reassuringly, though it felt hollow and fake, before he spun on his heel and bolted into the corridor once more, ignoring the narrowed eyes of the nurse, who was now sitting at the station in the middle of the ward clearly unimpressed by his commotion and the disturbance to the other patients on the ward. He rushed toward her. "Excuse me?"

"Yes?" the woman waved her hands down, shushing him.

Trent couldn't seem to control his rising voice. "Has Holly Hendricks been in this morning to see her mother?"

The nurse shook her head. "You're Mrs. Hendricks's first guests."

"Are you sure?" Trent asked.

"Of course." the woman snapped, slightly less friendly now. "I would have had to buzz her in. And we keep a log of everyone who enters the ward."

"Sorry, it's just that..." Trent backed up a step and then another. He would have taken off running if he knew where to go to look for her. "I have to find her."

"Holly would never miss being here with her mom as soon as she was able." Owen groaned from behind him.

"Take deep breaths, Trent." Lorenzo patted his arm. "Maybe she's exhausted and overslept."

Trent cut his stare to his best friends. There was no way he believed that bullshit.

He was already taking his phone from his pocket, then slipping out of the ICU so he could use it in the hallway as the rules permitted. He tapped Holly's icon on his frequently used contacts list and waited the eternity it took for it to ring and ring before dumping him to voicemail.

Obnoxious or not, he did it a few more times before also texting her, asking her to call.

"Something's wrong." His gaze flew to Lorenzo's then Owen's.

Neither man argued with him or told him he was overreacting. *Fuck!* He began to pace. His stomach knotted. "Should I call the police?"

"Call Andi first. See if she's heard from Holly." Owen suggested.

"Good idea." He punched in Reed's number, then waited impatiently. If Holly's best friend didn't know where she was, then no one would.

"Hey, Trent!"

"Sorry, dude. No time to chat. Where's your woman? I don't have her number, but I need to ask her something. It's urgent." Trent pinched the bridge of his nose. His only hope was that his "fake" wife had talked to one of her best friends about how badly he'd fucked up the night before. Embarrassing, yeah. But worth it if they could help him track Holly down and make sure she was okay.

"Oh. Uh, she's right here." Reed must have heard the alarm in his tone. He didn't even try to bust Trent's balls. "Hang on."

"Hello?" Andi asked, a laugh embedded in her greeting. "Having girl trouble?"

"How'd you know? Have you talked to Holly?" He would have pounced on her through the phone if he could have.

"Yeah. She told Kari and me that your dinner with her mom was a bit rocky." Andi answered, making the queasy feeling in his gut a million times worse.

Sure, that had only been yesterday evening. But so

much had happened since then, it seemed like a lifetime ago.

"Not after?" Trent asked again. "You haven't heard from her since then?"

"No. I assumed you two were...making up." She snorted. When she realized he wasn't laughing along with her, she got quiet. "Trent? What's going on? Is something wrong? You did apologize, right? Tell her that your head is shoved so far up your ass because you're freaked out about having a real relationship with her. Right?"

Was it that obvious to everyone else? Where did he start? "Holly's mom had her transplant last night."

"She did?" Andi's excitement at the news seemed kind of muffled by hurt.

"Yeah. Mrs. Hendricks got the news after the dinner disaster. I wasn't home. And then I was here, with her. And our phones had to be turned off. Everything moved so fast, it's all kind of a blur."

"Is her mom okay? How is Holly? Why are you calling? Oh no, something awful happened, didn't it?" Andi's imagination obviously had gotten the best of her.

"Yes. I think. Maybe." Trent was getting more confused by the second. If Andi didn't know any of this, then why was he talking to her? He needed information. And fast. Something was really screwed up. "But not with Mrs. Hendricks. She came through the surgery well. Holly was exhausted after the doctor let us know. We all were. We went home in the early morning and...well... things happened."

"Sex things?" Andi wondered.

"Yeah."

"With you, Holly, Lorenzo, *and* Owen, right?" She was catching on quick.

"Uh huh." Even now, remembering affected Trent despite the cold dread still hammering at his hindbrain. "But after, I fucked up again. I offered her more money to stay an extra three months."

"You did what?" Andi shrieked. "After you all had sex together? Trent, do you have any idea what that sounds like?"

"I do now." He groaned. "I can only say I was wrecked too and it seemed like a good idea at the time. She was worried about her mom's hospital bills and the rehab she's going to need. Extra stuff Holly hadn't counted on. I was trying to help."

"You're an idiot," Andi huffed.

"I know."

"So where is she now?"

Trent tried not to hyperventilate. "That's what I was hoping you could tell me. The ICU just opened to visitors. And she's not here."

"Oh fuck. Something *is* wrong."

In the background, Reed barked orders to Cooper to get Holly's other best friend, Kari, on the phone. It wasn't long before Andi was relaying the information Trent had shared with her and asking their mutual acquaintance the same questions.

"No luck, Trent. Kari doesn't know either. We're both blowing up Holly's phone right now. She's not answering us either." Andi sounded like she might cry. "So she was pissed when she left. Did she call a cab?"

"I don't know. I think she probably was more likely to just walk the mad off." He cursed, too guilty to admit she might have been more hurt than angry. "She wouldn't take any of us or even Moose with her. I think because she didn't plan to come back. What if..."

"No. Don't let your imagination run wild. We're going to find her, Trent." Andi didn't seem as certain about that as he would have liked. "Cooper's got Ford on the phone now."

That was good. Ford and Kari's other two guys were lawyers. Plus rich. If anyone could hunt someone down, it would be them. They had tons of resources and connections.

Trent looked at Owen and said, "Call the cops."

Then he slid down the wall, crumpled into a heap at its base. He didn't even realize he was praying until Lorenzo and knelt beside him and joined in. Owen stood guard over them both, his phone to his ear as he relayed the situation to the police in a calm manner Trent could never have managed right then. Hospital staff skirted around them in silence, respectful of their suffering, even if they mistook the reason behind it.

What if he never got to tell Holly all the things he should have said the night before?

In that moment, he swore that if he got the chance, he'd be as brave as she had been and admit that while their agreement might have started out for money, he was in it for a hell of a lot more than that now.

For love.

Feeling useless, he bolted to his feet, nearly cracking his skull against Lorenzo's in the process. "I can't sit here. I'm going to her house to see if she's there."

Even though in his gut he already knew she was gone, he had to be sure.

"I'll stay in case she comes back." Owen clapped Trent on the shoulder.

Lorenzo looked between them.

"Go ahead." Owen's mouth pinched at the corners,

making Trent aware it wasn't only him freaking out. It wouldn't only be him that suffered if... He couldn't allow himself to imagine the possibilities or he'd crumble again. "It's better if both of you look for Holly. The sooner we find her, the better."

At least they agreed on that.

2

———

"Trent, you're not going to like this," Brady—one of Kari's trio of lawyers—warned him as soon as he answered the phone two hours later. "And just so you know, everyone is here together, on speaker."

"As long as Holly's okay, it's fine. Just tell me what you found out." Trent held his breath as Lorenzo and Owen edged closer. They hadn't left his side for a moment of the thirty minutes since he'd slunk back to the hospital, defeated and without any more information than he'd had when he'd left.

Together, he and Lorenzo had nearly banged Holly's door down, gone to the police department to give them as much information as possible, checked with admissions at the hospital, scoured other medical facilities, and even contacted the home health aide they'd hired for Mrs. Hendricks, who'd confirmed that Holly hadn't returned to her mother's house the night before and—after using her key to verify—that she was still not there.

At least Trent was able to scrub the vision of Holly falling in the shower or having some other accident while alone in her home from his brain. That didn't leave a lot of other positive scenarios, though. Owen and Lorenzo were as invested in her as he was. So he too hit the speaker button on his phone.

"As your attorneys of record, we just received an email addressed to you." Ford cursed. "It's about Holly. In fact, it's a fucking ransom note."

"A what?" Trent shouted as a ringing started in his ears and grew louder, threatening to drown out the rest of the world. Lorenzo braced him, or maybe supported himself against Trent. Either way, they held each other up as Owen turned and punched the wall. He didn't seem to notice the blood welling on his battered knuckles.

"Someone nabbed her. They want half of your inheritance in exchange for her safe return." Josh practically spat the information.

"They took her? Because of me? My father's dirty money?" Trent thought he might pass out, so he bent in half and planted his palms on his knees. "I should have known better than to take it. It has never gotten me anything good. Only screwed things up worse."

"What do you want us to do?" Ford asked.

"Give them anything they want. Just get her back." Was that even really a question? Trent lifted his head to see if he was nuts, but Owen and Lorenzo were leveling similar bewildered glares at the phone Trent clutched.

"Look, Trent. It might not be that easy. We have Bronson here." Brady was talking, but Trent was having a hard time listening. All he could think about was how scared Holly must be, if she was even still alive.

No, he couldn't allow himself to imagine that she wasn't or he'd lose it.

"Who?" he mumbled.

"He's the head of our security team," Ford explained. "He said you should never negotiate with these sorts of people."

"I don't give a fuck!" Trent bellowed. "We have to get her back. Now!"

"We will." Unlike usual, Josh wasn't joking around. "In fact, we already sent our jet to pick up a few guys who can help."

"Who?" Trent hoped he said Superman. Because no one else was going to make him feel better. Holly was in harm's way, and it was his damn fault. Holy fuck. If anything happened to her...

All because of his father's fortune.

Trent never should have touched it. And now the only woman he'd ever loved was going to be the one to pay.

"Lucas used to work for the government, in a no-name agency. JRad is a tech genius for the OHPD who does consulting on the side. Jordan is the head of a private security firm specializing in black ops type shit, and Ransom, Sevan, and Levi work for him. They've all been in situations worse than this and survived."

"*Worse than this*?" Trent was about to lose it. "That isn't possible."

"Put it this way, all of them have been through situations where lives of their spouses were at risk and managed to get them back. They understand what you're going through both from a tactical and emotional perspective."

"When will they arrive?" Owen asked when Trent was too overwhelmed to do it.

"Ninety minutes," Brady responded for Team Lawyers. "That's still well ahead of the deadline set by the blackmailers."

"When will they give her back? Can we make it sooner?" Lorenzo nearly vibrated with tension from his place beside Trent and Owen.

"The meeting is set for two, but we'll see what the experts say." That seemed like an eternity from now. Trent needed a plan B. What if these guys weren't as good as Ford thought? Or what if the assholes who'd stolen Holly didn't play by the rules?

"Call the bank. Or whoever the fuck you have to. Get the cash, set it up. If your gang gets here in time to help, fine. But those bastards can have anything they want from me, so long as they release Holly unharmed."

"I understand." Ford was grim. "I can't say I'd feel different if it was Kari in danger."

"And after we have Holly back, we'll have a chance to do our worst in return," Bronson growled in the background.

Owen flexed his bloody fist and Lorenzo bared his teeth in a snarl that should have terrified Trent, yet somehow made him feel better, if only for a moment.

"What are you going to do about Holly's mom?" Andi asked.

Lorenzo spoke up then. "Nothing. They sedated her when they realized she wasn't going to remain calmly in bed while her daughter was missing. Hopefully, by the time the drugs wear off, this will be a bad memory."

Trent squeezed his nose between his thumb and forefinger. "Thank you for your help. I honestly don't know what we'd do without you guys."

"It was the least we could do. We feel somewhat responsible given our role in this. *When* you get her back, you have to tell Holly what's between you has nothing to do with your dumbass contract anymore." Cooper groaned. "Hell, we could see that night it was already more than an arranged marriage or we never would have done it."

"You're right." Trent looked first at Owen, then Lorenzo. "It is. It was. It always has been. And as soon as I can, I'm going to make sure Holly understands that too."

Lorenzo extended his fist, so Trent bumped it before Owen added his own.

They were in this together. All they needed now was for Holly to be returned safely and with her heart still open to theirs.

3

———

Holly writhed, twisting her wrists against the plastic zip ties holding them. Just a little more and...

Yes! She finally felt her arm, buzzing with pins and needles, slick with what she assumed was blood, slip from the restraint. She winced as she rotated her wrists and brought them around in front of her, things cracking and popping, as stiff as if she were eighty years old.

It was so dark that white spots like static fizzled in her vision as her body tried desperately to make out even a hint of her surroundings. It was no use. She'd probably been locked in the trunk of this thankfully new and clean-smelling car—probably rented—for at least an hour.

At first it had been all she could do to keep from having a panic attack as she crashed into the walls of the tiny space every time they took a corner at what seemed like breakneck speeds. She'd hit her head and lain there, dazed, for a while until she realized that they were no longer moving.

Muffled voices were followed by the thud of two car

doors shutting. They'd left. Both of the men who'd captured her and were attempting to use her as a bargaining chip. Too bad they didn't know Trent or how determined he was to spend his father's inheritance on something that would make the world a better place. Accessible clean energy and efficient, low-cost batteries to store it would be something worth dying for, if it came to that.

No. Hell no. Holly refused to think those things.

Instead, she closed her eyes and pretended it was dark by choice as she took deep, measured breaths and imagined happy stuff, like Kari's engagement party, giving Moose treats, and...okay, fine...her budding relationship with Trent, Owen, and Lorenzo.

What she wouldn't give for a hug from one or all three of them right then.

There would be plenty of time to figure things out between them after she escaped from the psychos holding her hostage. Because if nothing else, the careless disregard those assholes had shown for her made her realize that no matter what dumb shit had come out of Trent's mouth the night before, he wasn't like the barbarians who'd captured her.

He cared about more than just the money.

Even if he was too gun-shy to admit it, even to himself.

Holly gritted her teeth, determined to make it out of this mess so that she could tell Trent she wasn't going to give up on him until he recognized the value of what they had. Owen or Lorenzo too. She wanted to get to know them better, to open her heart to them like she had her body.

But none of that could happen if she didn't save herself first.

Fuck waiting for someone else to do it for her, for these men to get their shit together or for her friends to figure out something had gone horribly wrong and dispatch the cavalry, which she absolutely believed they would if they realized she was missing. Nope, she'd taken care of herself, and her mom, for years now despite the universe conspiring against them. She didn't need help. She would make those assholes pay for stealing her and taking her away just when her mother needed her most.

Once she'd gotten herself good and mad, Holly used every bit of her fear as kindling to light a fire within herself. She prepared to fight.

Those bastards! How dare they treat her like this? She kicked the backseat as hard as she could, over and over, but nothing happened. So she used her fingers, which were regaining feeling, to search for some sort of lever. It took her minutes, too many considering she didn't know when her abductors would return, to methodically search every inch of the fuzzy fabric lining the back of the seats and the area around them.

No luck. Weren't cars these days supposed to have safety features? What the hell?

Holly groaned as she writhed, finally managing to turn herself over to face the rear of the trunk.

And that's when she saw it.

A faint, slime-green square. It glowed in the dark as bright as the beam of a lighthouse slicing through a storm to her fully dilated eyes. It took some more wriggling, a smashed elbow, and a steady stream of curses, but Holly managed to maneuver herself so that she could nearly reach it.

Her fingertips brushed the lever.

She tried again, straining and forcing her poor hands

to function. When she made contact, she tugged. The trunk popped open.

Holly nearly fainted at the wave of dizziness and relief that washed over her.

But what if the men who'd abducted her were waiting outside?

A wedge of sunlight blasted through the opening and stabbed her in the eyes. She scrunched them nearly closed and fumbled around until she half-crawled, half-tumbled from the trunk onto pavement. Holly grabbed the bumper to help lever herself mostly upright, her entire body screaming as she stretched.

Blind in the searing sun, she stumbled, her hands outstretched as if she were a zombie, moving as fast as she could toward the din of people and traffic in the distance. She scrambled although she had no idea where she was or where she was going. So long as it was the opposite direction from her captors, she was good with that.

Tripping over something, maybe a curb, she went down hard on one knee then shot to her feet, shouting, "Help! Someone, help me!"

Blinking rapidly, she tried to bring her surroundings into focus. Before she could, Holly crashed hard into a solid wall of man. She screamed and thrashed, refusing to allow them to take her back to the dark trunk. Next time she wouldn't escape.

"I've got you!" Strong arms banded around her.

It was the smell of vanilla aftershave mixed with solder that made her pause right before she kneed him in the nuts. She croaked, "T-Trent?"

"Yeah. Yeah, it's me. I've got you. I'm so sorry, Holly. Are you okay?"

Every single one of her bones dissolved. It was him.

And only one thing made sense. If he knew where they'd be, that meant he'd come to buy her freedom. Even if it had required giving up his fortune *and* his dream. Because she'd seen his budget. If he gave the blackmailers what they'd told her they were going to demand from him—half of the big fat pile of gold his dad had left him—the remainder wasn't enough to get where he wanted to go.

Holly's vision cleared until she could make out the briefcase he had apparently dropped in order to catch her. It had cracked open, and wads of hundreds spilled from within.

"The money! Take it, Trent. Run. Before they get it *and* you." She squirmed again. This time to save him, not herself.

Because that's what love was about, wasn't it?

Even after everything that had happened the day before, and the danger she'd been in, the most frequent thought she'd had during the endless night was about Trent and the position he'd be in if he had to choose between her and his fledgling company. The damage it would do to him either way would be devastating. Maybe, just maybe, they could fix this.

Right then, a man with a prosthetic running hook bolted past her, far faster than she could have managed with both of her natural feet. He clutched a gun and shouted at someone to stop. Holly couldn't see who he was yelling at because several other men surrounded her and Trent, Owen and Lorenzo among them, and shoved both of them to the ground over top of the cash.

Safe. Her body had survived. So had his fortune.

But what about their future together, and their hearts?

4

———

"Holly!" Trent bellowed, and careened toward her, dropping the briefcase full of money he'd intended to exchange for her freedom, so he could scoop her up sooner. He couldn't believe she was right there. Within reach.

In that moment, the bullshit he'd tried to convince himself of when he'd watched her walk out of his home was proven false. Only having her in his arms was going to make him whole again. Fortunately, Holly seemed to agree. Or at least she preferred him to the monsters who'd attacked her. That was a pretty low bar, but he'd take it.

She flew to him and slammed into his chest. By the time his arms came around her, two more shadows fell over them: Lorenzo and Owen.

They bristled as they faced out, protecting them from anyone who might be following.

Lucas raced past, thundering toward the man with dark glasses and a ball cap, who'd been circling the drop spot Trent had been approaching, despite the advice of the specialty team Ford and his friends had mustered to get Holly back.

Trent hadn't even known guys like that existed in real life. Super spies who'd seen more shit than he could imagine. He would be perfectly happy to return to his boring, everyday life after a glimpse at what they dealt with on the regular.

Next thing he knew, he was being shoved to the ground along with Holly. He blanketed her smaller body and felt Lorenzo and Owen do the same, sheltering them both as two other agents—Jordan and Ransom—stood back to back, booted feet spread, weapons drawn.

The screech of tires and the wail of sirens, trailing off as good guys raced after the blackmailers, reassured Trent that their protectiveness was probably unnecessary. The immediate danger faded.

A clicking from beneath him made Trent tense. He ran his hands over Holly, who shook uncontrollably, making her teeth chatter as she tried to summon some smartass comment to cover up her terror.

The whoosh of relief slamming through him made his stomach feel like it turned inside out. His face went hot and his head spun. All he wanted was to get Holly somewhere safe. Somewhere he could make sure she was protected before he tried to fix the damage he'd done.

As Lorenzo and Owen got to their feet, dusting off their jeans, he did too. He scooped Holly up and turned, heading toward the rest of the agents and police officers who streamed from vans and buildings nearby as if someone had kicked their nest. One of them could get the money. All he cared about was Holly. She clung to his shoulders, burying her face in his neck as he climbed into the open back of a plain white commercial van. Despite its innocuous appearance from the outside, the inside was loaded with gear and weapons and who knew what else his new friends needed to save the world. Including their resident nerd mastermind, JRad.

Trent took a seat on a bench against one of the walls, cradling Holly as he did.

It kind of freaked him out that she didn't resist or even protest.

Lorenzo and Owen were right behind them. They settled across from him and Holly, shoulder to shoulder. Someone closed the door from the outside with a deafening clang. Holly shuddered.

"It's just us now. We've got you." Lorenzo promised, leaning forward to rub her back.

Holly nodded. "Reminded me of the trunk lid slamming on those fuckers' car. They locked me inside."

"Wrap her in this." JRad, wearing a high-tech headset quit toying with a computer that had three screens long enough to extend a blanket to Owen.

Holly recoiled, leaning away from the stranger and closer to Owen, Lorenzo, and Trent.

Owen accepted it and worked with Trent to tuck it around her. "Thanks, man."

When Holly felt Owen's hand on her, snuggling her into the soft fabric, she relaxed, settling against Trent's body. Lorenzo leaned in and adjusted the fabric on her other side, covering her legs as well as possible in the tight space.

"Are you okay, Holly?" Trent scanned as much of her as he could see, which wasn't much considering there wasn't so much as a molecule of air between them.

"I think so." Did she mean to brush her lips across his neck when she said that?

Trent swallowed a groan. She reached up and cupped his cheek, as if reassuring herself that he was real and that he was there. If he had his way, he'd never leave her alone again.

"She's bleeding." Lorenzo cursed in Portuguese.

Holly tried to reassure them it was nothing, but she sat a bit too still as Lorenzo fetched a paramedic, then hovered as the woman checked Holly before bandaging her bruised and cut wrists. Miraculously, it seemed that was the worst of her injuries. At least the physical ones.

Trent wished they could take her home right then and talk in private about any of the wounds that went deeper than her flesh, including ones he may have inflicted himself.

They sat there as she recounted being abducted to the authorities. When the officer asked her if she'd experienced any sexual assault, Owen bent in half as if someone had punched him in the gut.

"No, I'm fine. They must really have wanted Trent's money." Holly reached out and touched the cop's hand lightly. "I've told you every detail I can remember several times. Please, may I go? I just want to rest and call my mom so she knows—"

Holly's face blanched of what little color had returned to her cheeks. Lorenzo steadied her until Trent could put his arms around her and tuck her against his chest again.

"Oh shit. I'm the worst daughter ever." A tear slid down Holly's cheek then. "Trent, how is my mom?"

"She's doing great." He smiled wryly. "She might never forgive me for losing you, but...other than that, better than expected. The doctors sedated her because she was ready to come out here and kick some ass to get you back."

Holly snorted at that. "You're right. She sounds fine.

Thank God. I can't believe I didn't ask you sooner." She went limp in his hold.

Trent said, "She's had enough."

The policewoman looked up at him and nodded, then asked Jordan, the head of the security team, "You want to take them or should I get them a ride?"

"We'll take them. We're going to hang around a while."

"I'll hire you to protect her, at least until we can set up something long-term." Trent was grateful for their help.

"No need. Westbrook, Armand, and King law firm already did." Jordan grinned. "And they tip really well."

"Just like that? We can walk out of here?" Holly asked.

"Where you go from here is up to you." Jordan nodded, looking between the four of them. "I mean, I'd recommend you stay vigilant and don't go anywhere alone. Other than that, just let me know where your home base is going to be and we'll set up as many precautions as we can to keep you safe."

"I want to see my mom." Holly didn't hesitate.

"Unfortunately, the sedation protocol also means no visitors so she can rest undisturbed. The nurse said it's a twenty-four hour ban and that they'll allow her to wake naturally in the morning," Owen told her. "Until then, you should rest."

"Oh, I..." Holly looked at Owen and Lorenzo, then to Trent. "Where should I go?"

"What do you want to happen from here?" he wondered. Had he ruined everything or would she give him another chance? He didn't deserve it, but he'd grab it anyway if she offered.

"I want you to take me home."

Lorenzo dropped his head and Owen balled his fists. Though Trent tried to hide his disappointment, it must have been obvious in his frown and the way his arms went slack around Holly. "Okay."

"To *your* house, I mean," she said quietly, sparking hope within him.

"Oh. Really?" He froze, afraid to so much as breathe lest she change her mind.

"Yeah. If that's what you want too. Or are you still going to insist, like last night, that you don't care about anything other than super-hot foursomes and finishing the work we started together." Holly jabbed her finger into his chest and stood up. She flicked her gaze toward their new bodyguards. Though Jordan wisely acted like he hadn't heard what she'd confessed, the slight tilt to his lips made it clear he had and that he didn't disapprove. Of course, Trent, Lorenzo, and Owen had heard all about how he wasn't exactly traditional when it came to his relationship, and he'd bragged about his own feisty wife and their lover more than once in the short time since they'd met him, but Holly didn't know that.

And Trent hadn't done much to convince her that what they had was everything to him.

That was bullshit. Time to own it and fix it.

Not only for him and Holly, but also for Lorenzo and Owen, who were frozen enough to resemble mannequins while observing their exchange.

"No, Holly. I'm not going to be that stupid ever again. I want this every bit as much as you do. And the reasons why have nothing to do with dollars and cents. Hell, I would have given it up to get you back and considered that the best deal of all time."

She bit her lip, then glanced over at Lorenzo and Owen.

Owen kicked Lorenzo's boot with his own sneaker,

making him jump. "Yeah. That's what I want, too. All three of us do. We never want you to leave again."

Trent winced, thinking of how her departure had been salt in Lorenzo's clearly unhealed wounds. He would damn the woman who'd left his friend at the altar, but then they would never have met and have formed the bond that was about to change their lives forever.

"How about we take it one night at a time?" Holly sighed. "I'm not ready to think about the future. For now, all I can focus on is being free, here with you. I want you to surround me again and make me feel safe and warm."

Trent could see the rest of what she left unsaid hanging between them.

That's what she wanted, *even if it meant getting hurt later.*

Well, that wasn't going to happen. Not if he had any say in how things played out.

From the looks Lorenzo and Owen were shooting his way, they all had the same thing in mind.

They needed a do over on the night before.

He wasn't about to fuck up their second chance.

5

———

Owen chewed his thumbnail as he peered into the visor mirror from the passenger seat of one of the unmarked sedans Jordan and his team had commandeered. Holly was sandwiched between Lorenzo and Trent on the backseat of the vehicle as they sped toward their house.

Thank God she was okay.

Relatively. He'd seen the terror in her eyes, which darted around every few seconds, as if making sure no one was going to reclaim her and try to sell her back to them.

He hated the fact that even if he'd wanted to, he couldn't have met the blackmailers' demands. Sure, he'd wished he'd been born loaded like Trent a million times in his life—had even dreamed about it on the nights he'd gone without anything to eat growing up, or the year and a half he'd spent living under a railway trestle on the outskirts of town. That had been before Trent had stumbled across his turf on an urban hike with Moose, helped him get a job, and eventually invited him to be

33

roommates. But never before had he realized how woefully inadequate what he had to offer someone was compared to men like Trent, or Ford, Brady, and Josh for that matter.

All he had to give was himself. And maybe a handful of orgasms, which Holly could get from any guy lucky enough to be welcomed into her bed.

Since she'd escaped, she'd been glued to Trent. It made sense. After all, he was the one she cared about. He and Lorenzo were simply guests in their bed, toys to make their sex even better. He felt like a leech. And yet he knew that if she asked for all three of them when they turned this next corner and walked into their house together, he'd be right there.

Because he was weak. Being needed was his kryptonite. No one had ever needed him for shit before. And though he didn't have money, he could give her a whole lot of himself if she would accept it. He'd never been able to count on someone before Trent, and if he could repay his friend while also making his best friend's girlfriend happy, then Owen was in despite the risks he was taking with his own feelings.

He ground his teeth as he watched Lorenzo caress Holly's hair and murmur foreign shit to her that sounded sexy, even to him. Trent had cash and his romantic side. Lorenzo brought the spice. What the fuck did Owen have to add to their arrangement?

Nothing.

Would he be left out in the cold, like always, when Holly realized that too?

Owen gripped his knee so hard his knuckles turned white. When Jordan glanced over and raised a brow in question, he shook his head. This was fine. Everything was fine.

Or at least it would be if he didn't let his demons get the best of him. What had happened the night before, when Trent let his past overcome his better sense, had showed Owen the dangers of getting choked by his hang-ups. He had to avoid making the same mistake.

He was completely out of his element, in over his head. But he had to figure out how to act like a normal guy who knew how to care for someone else and let them do the same for him. And he had to do it fast.

Before Owen was entirely ready, Jordan pulled into their driveway. Moose barked his head off as they spilled out of the car. He was probably pissed at being left behind, or maybe just glad to see them reunited.

I know, buddy, me too, he thought to the dog. Hell, even that he owed to Holly. She'd found the puppy and given him to Trent to look after. The animal had been the first "person" Owen had ever fully trusted. Then Trent had proven that sometimes decent people did decent things for those around them.

And now Holly...

Owen refused to get too far ahead of himself until he knew where he, and Lorenzo, stood with her.

Surrounded by the guys and Jordan, Holly made her way up their sidewalk and into the house. As expected, Moose danced around her feet, licking her hand and bringing back the easy smile that had been missing from her face since they'd offended her the night before.

Owen shut the door behind them, leaving Jordan and the rest of his team, who were already in place to strategize about how best to secure their home. He couldn't say he minded after seeing what some people would do for a piece of Trent's newfound stash.

Trent and Lorenzo guided Holly to the sofa, where she plopped down and leaned forward to hug the dog. "I'm so glad to see you, Moose."

When her voice cracked, Owen had to take action. If he stood there and watched her break down, he'd lose it too. And right now, he needed to keep his own shit together. He'd have to wait until she was okay, however long that took, before they could deal with his—and Lorenzo's—building tension.

He looked at his friend, who swallowed hard before giving him a slight nod. Yeah, Lorenzo knew exactly how Owen felt.

They had to trust that Trent was going to make this right for them all, and that wasn't a position either of them was used to being in. Having always fended for themselves, it frustrated the hell out of him.

Rather than risk losing his patience, he tried to help in some small way.

"When's the last time you ate?" Owen asked. He might not be a gourmet-chef-in-disguise like Trent, but he could heat a bowl of soup or cut up an apple or something.

Trent sank onto the cushion next to her, putting his hand on her knee, while Lorenzo manned his post standing near the arm of the couch. He couldn't relax enough to lounge. Owen didn't blame the guy.

"Dinner last night." Holly held her hand up, palm out when he turned toward the kitchen. "But...I'm really not hungry. Food isn't what I need right now."

"You're exhausted." Lorenzo hummed as if he was going to sing her a lullaby.

"I am, but I don't think I could fall asleep either. There

are too many things still racing through my mind. Too much nervous energy making me restless." She shifted before blinking up at Trent.

Owen knew how to take care of that. But he wasn't about to be the one to suggest it. Neither did his best friend. Was Trent going to falter again, even in the face of what Holly was obviously begging for?

Owen could picture them, soothing each other, skin on skin. Erasing the terror of the past several hours and replacing it with mind-blanking pleasure. He could do that for her a hell of a lot better than he could provide sustenance. Or maybe that was just a different kind of nourishment.

Trent lifted his hand to stroke her hair, but his fingers stopped short, trembling in the air as if he was afraid of hurting her again.

Holly leaned into his touch, connecting them when Trent hesitated.

She was exactly what they needed, and Owen wanted to be the same for her. Even if it was only temporary, or as the second—or third—string player in her love life. All he cared about was erasing some of the doubt and trepidation in her pretty eyes.

"I need you. All three of you." Holly wiped a tear from her cheek, making him want to go back and rip the bastards who'd taken her from then to shreds. "Can we have a repeat of last night? Except change the ending? Pretend none of it happened? I mean, everything after the sex stuff. Try again and see if we can get it right this time?"

"I'd like nothing more than that." Trent groaned. "I fucked up, Holly. I should have—"

"Don't tell me what you should have done. Do it now

instead." She rose, and Owen shuffled closer. Lorenzo and Trent were right there with him.

Holly reached out to him.

So he went.

Consequences be damned.

6
___

Owen shed his clothes before he'd even crossed the threshold of Trent's room.

Lorenzo kicked his jeans into the corner with a flick worthy of his profession as one of Vegas's most popular male strippers. Owen didn't possess Trent's sophistication, or Lorenzo's suave moves, but he had a burning desire to make Holly feel like he never had before. Wanted, cherished, protected, and—as long as he didn't have to say the words—loved.

She deserved it.

The way she'd sacrificed so much of her own life to care for her mother, and her willingness to volunteer to help Trent the night his father had died, and how she'd rescued Moose, not to mention the affection she'd lavished on Trent, Lorenzo, and himself...

Well, he may not have known her long, but she'd shown them the kind of person she was and the quality of her soul. It couldn't have been more attractive to him. Having her in their home, and now in their beds, had brought them all together.

The fact that she didn't seem to realize how much she had to offer only made him want to prove it to her that much more.

Trent paused at the side of the bed. How the man resisted climbing in next to Holly, Owen would never understand. "Are you sure about this? You've been through a lot. I don't want to rush things and risk turning stuff between us into a bigger disaster."

"That's not possible, jerk." Lorenzo put his hand on Trent's lower back and shoved.

Holly laughed when Trent toppled onto her before shooting Lorenzo a glare. The sound did something to Owen, and it seemed like his two friends, too.

It calmed him, made him think they maybe had gotten incredibly lucky and that somehow, things were going to be okay.

Holly was going to recover from her ordeal. So were they, and maybe their relationship, too.

At least he hoped it could be possible.

So he didn't wait. He got into Trent's bed on Holly's right side as Lorenzo mirrored him on her left.

"For the record..." Holly murmured as she spread her legs to make room for Trent between them while also reaching out, searching blindly for Owen and Lorenzo. "I *am* sure. As sure as I was last night. No, even more. Because you came for me. You actually came."

Her voice hitched at that last bit, and Owen had to resist the urge to smack Trent for making her doubt they would for even a moment.

"Of course I did." Trent seemed slightly insulted she'd consider anything else, but why should he be when that's the impression he'd given her?

Hopefully, she'd known that Owen and Lorenzo wouldn't have allowed Trent to do anything but barter for her. They would have done it themselves if they'd had the necessary cash. And if Ford hadn't hired the security experts, Owen probably would have pulled out some of the dirty tricks he'd learned on the street and found a way to talk to people he'd thought best left forgotten in order to track her down.

Fortunately, it hadn't come to that so she didn't realize how savage he could be when backed into a corner.

"Thanks," Holly whispered before spearing her fingers into Trent's hair and dragging him to her for a slow, tender kiss. If Owen hadn't already been hard—a reaction to the adrenaline, or maybe the direction he'd hoped they were headed all along—he would have gotten stiff watching the way they made out. It was entirely different from how Trent had been with women they'd shared before. Hell, he'd never kissed them at all. Even if he had, Owen was sure it wouldn't have been with as much intimacy or passion.

Owen hoped to experience that kind of affection someday, but for now, binging on their passion would work. If his fist dropped to his cock and began to stroke it, no one would blame him. Certainly not Lorenzo, who did the same as he stared at the pair between them, gluing them together.

Owen lowered himself to his stomach and brushed his thumb right below the bandage encircling Holly's wrist. The sight of it pained him, so he leaned in to place gentle kisses above the gauze and tape, traveling up her arm. Lorenzo looked at him over Trent's back and proceeded to mimic his motions.

They worked together, pretending they were trying to soothe her when Owen knew damn well it was themselves they were comforting. They'd barely found her and they'd almost lost her. Their friendship wouldn't have been able to recover if anything had happened to her.

They'd almost ruined everything.

Owen wasn't going to let that happen again. She was precious to him, even if she didn't understand that yet.

Holly shivered and wrenched her mouth from Trent's in order to suck in several heaving breaths. She whipped her gaze to Owen. "Whatever you're doing, don't stop."

He grinned. He was worshipping her. So was Lorenzo. Trent would be again too, as soon as he finished ridding himself of his clothes. While he did, Owen walked Holly's T-shirt up her stomach and nuzzled the underside of her breasts. She was so soft and warm he couldn't wait until he could sink into her and burn off his lingering tension.

Lorenzo lifted her shoulders and helped him shed her shirt and unwrap her bra from around her luscious body. When Trent returned, pressing his bare chest to hers, she gasped. "Hurry, Trent."

Owen slid his hand between them. There wasn't going to be enough time to do this the way he would have preferred. So instead, he concentrated on making sure she was ready and able to handle it when Trent lifted up enough to fit his cock to her entrance.

He traced light circles around her clit and sucked on her nipple while Lorenzo took care of her other side, kneading her breast and taking up kissing her when Trent levered himself farther upright for a better angle.

Holly's moan made it clear when he'd worked his way inside her tight pussy.

The guy had more self-control than Owen. He started

out with slow, gentle glides of his hips that plunged him to the hilt before slipping back out. But it didn't take long before Trent was obeying the urging of Holly's heels on his ass, which insisted he drive deeper and faster within her.

Owen glanced up and saw Trent fucking with his eyes closed, a sure sign that he was trying to hold out. Owen didn't blame him. Holly looked incredible taking his dick and loving every second of the time they spent joined.

So it shocked the hell out of him when Holly said, "Trent, don't stop. I'm close."

And instead of reassuring her that he was too, he cooed, "Go ahead. Get it, Holly. I want you to come on me."

How the hell was he going to pull that off without caving to his own desires? Owen and Lorenzo shot each other questioning stares over Holly's body, which writhed between them. Lorenzo asked, "You're not gonna join her?"

"Not if I can help it." Trent grunted as he drove forward.

Holly froze, a moment away from climax. "Huh?"

"Not this time anyway. Next time, probably." Trent grabbed one of her knees in each palm and rocked them back so he could plunge all the way in.

Holly seemed like she might argue, except the combination of Trent's drilling cock, Owen's hand stroking her clit, and Lorenzo reclaiming her mouth with his own made it impossible. Every muscle in her body tensed. From this close, Owen watched her pussy clamp around Trent's shaft before she fed her scream to Lorenzo and shuddered between them.

Trent tried to ride it out, to let her take her fill, but he had to bail at the last minute. "Fuck, Holly. It feels too good."

He rolled to the side toward Lorenzo and shoved their friend's shoulder in Holly's direction. His meaning was clear even if he was rendered speechless by trying to keep his desire in check.

Holly was still surrendering small, evenly spaced moans and sighs when Lorenzo took Trent's place and rubbed his dick up and down her slick slit. Her eyes flew open and her mouth formed a tempting O as she caught on to Trent's diabolical plan.

When she nodded, and held her hand out toward Lorenzo, he gave her what she wanted.

The man dropped a string of Portuguese that was probably part curse and part thanks as he invaded her still pulsing pussy, surrounding himself in her heat and softness.

The thing about Lorenzo was that he had nerves of steel and all the self-control that Owen lacked. He'd see this as a challenge. Owen grinned and settled in for the show.

"You think this is funny?" Holly asked with a wry grin.

"When it's them you're torturing, yeah." He laughed, then wrapped his hand around the back of her neck, leaning down to seal their mouths in a kiss. He hadn't meant for it to be so explosive, but when she met him halfway they collided, their lips crashing against each other as they took what they needed.

He'd wanted to do that from the moment they'd recovered her from the blackmailers. Waiting for hours, and acting like they didn't have this intense bond between them, had nearly wrecked him all over again.

"Yeah!" Trent cheered them on. "Get her ready again so Lorenzo can make her even hotter for your turn."

Owen growled, the anticipation of having her only ramping him up higher. But first, Lorenzo was going to pamper her and give her a break. They all knew Owen wasn't capable of that kind of patience and gentleness.

He backed away, busying himself with caressing every inch of her that he could reach from his side of the bed while Trent did the same from his, kissing her shoulder and telling her over and over again how great she'd felt wrapped around him and how hard he was going to come when he finally allowed himself to surrender.

Lorenzo smiled down at her when her eyes finally fluttered open again. He cuddled her in his arms and rubbed his cheek against hers. His hair fell across their faces, curtaining them from Trent and Owen. With a sense of false privacy, he murmured, "Hi."

"Hey," she smiled contentedly.

Maybe Trent had been enough for her. Owen and Lorenzo wouldn't blame her if he had.

"You're not going to leave me like this are you?" she murmured.

"Like what?" he wondered.

"Needy. Hoping for more..."

"I'll give you as much as I can," Lorenzo promised. Would she realize, as Owen did, that he was talking about a lot more than a ride on his dick? Holly had reached the real Trent and brought him out from behind a wall they'd never been able to break through. It hadn't taken her long to get to each of them, even if she had no idea of how special that was. Lorenzo was hooked too. If he couldn't say so, he was about to let his body do the talking for him.

"Good. I can take it, Lorenzo."

Did she realize what Lorenzo suspected? He'd confessed to Trent and Owen one drunken night that he believed the reason his almost-bride hadn't showed up to their wedding had been because she couldn't handle Lorenzo's desires. That he never should have risked sharing her with a friend they'd grown up with, not even if she'd been the one to plant the idea in his mind.

Lorenzo had heard they'd ended up together and somehow genuinely hoped those backstabbers were happy, even though her one-time fantasy—which may have been a ploy to test-drive the other man—had triggered something in Lorenzo that he'd never been able to shake.

Owen prayed, for Lorenzo's sake if not his own, that Holly wouldn't decide later she'd checked a foursome off her sexual bucket list and leave them with only memories of how incredible an encounter like this could be with no way to ever achieve these heights again.

Lorenzo must have been sharing Owen's thoughts. His cock wilted slightly. Of course, Holly noticed. "Need a break? Or maybe a hand...or mouth?"

He shook his head. "No, I only need you and this silky pussy."

"Quit thinking and fuck," Trent commanded. "Don't let your doubts ruin the best thing we've ever had. Trust me, it's a terrible idea."

Lorenzo nodded then seemed to allow physical sensations to overwhelm him. It was the only way to guarantee he didn't let his issues trip them up like Trent's had the night before. Owen vowed he would do the same when it was his turn.

Holly hummed when Lorenzo ground them together then withdrew to begin again. From either side of them,

Trent and Owen witnessed how she molded to him, wrapping her arms and legs around him to hold him tight. Lorenzo wasn't going to reject her full-body hug. He got lost in the feel of her surrounding him, clinging to him, instead of shoving him away like his ex had.

That meant he moved more carefully, with shorter, slower strokes. And as amazing as Holly must have felt against and around him, he had enough stamina to last a long time with such measured movements.

Holly, on the other hand, wasn't complaining. She ran her fingers through Lorenzo's hair, dragged him to her for long, languid kisses that matched the sedate pace of their movements, and sighed between his open lips. She rallied from her previous climax bit by bit until eventually she was digging her heels into his ass and encouraging him to fuck her faster and harder, though it would have been impossible for him to be any deeper inside her than he already was.

Owen stared at when her body swallowed Lorenzo whole. Damn.

Trent lifted her hand and kissed each of her fingers before asking, "Are you going to come again, Holly?"

She bit her lip and nodded as she concentrated on the pleasure beginning to coalesce in her core. Owen saw her tightening around Lorenzo, and wondered if he was going to be able to resist, like Trent had. He was sure his roommate would have loved to surrender, to allow himself to be swept away with her, except he knew—as Owen did —that the longer they held out, the better they could satisfy Holly.

And they had a lot to make up for after the night before.

That thought alone kept him focused, primed without danger of being unable to do his part.

Lorenzo put every one of the hip rolls dancing had taught him to good use as he fucked Holly. When he tapped a particular spot deep within her, she gasped and her eyes flew open. He grinned as he repeated the motion again and again.

Trent chuckled. "You're evil, Lorenzo."

"Determined," he corrected through clenched teeth.

It only took a time or two more before Holly shattered around him. He let her squeeze his cock and hug it tight before he admitted he was about to lose it too and reluctantly withdrew.

It was only when he slumped onto the pillows that he seemed to realize what his marathon performance had done to Owen, who was nearly vibrating with the need to be inside Holly. The tip of his cock was wet with precome and his breathing was harsh and uneven.

Owen had run out of patience and restraint. He rasped to Trent, "Make sure I don't hurt her."

"You're not going to do that." Holly grabbed hold of his wrist and yanked. "I don't know what's wrong with me today, but...I need more. I need you."

"I don't see anything wrong with that at all." Trent grinned even as Owen grimaced. Was she bummed that her body craved his?

When he hesitated, she lost the dazed look in her eyes long enough to rethink what she'd said. "Owen, sorry. I didn't mean it like it sounded. It's just that I've never been like this before. You guys make me...insatiable."

"It's because you want all three of us. Together again. And until you have it, this is just an appetizer." Trent kissed her forehead. "I know, because it's the same for me."

Sure enough, Trent was so damn hard it had to hurt. Lorenzo was too, idly rubbing his dick while he watched Holly move restlessly on the bed beneath Owen. Every stroke or two Lorenzo had to stop and let himself recover some more. Owen could understand. Holly had him on the verge of exploding and he hadn't even been inside her yet.

"We can do that if you want." Owen tried not to sound disappointed. Selfish or not, he'd hoped to have her to himself for just a few minutes before they moved on.

Holly shook her head. "Trent's going to have to wait his damn turn."

The guy chuckled at that, clearly not too upset about it. "Every turn is my turn when I get to see you loving this like you do."

"Good. Then it's settled. Please, Owen." Her doe eyes seemed bigger and more beautiful than he'd realized when she peered up at him from beneath heavy lids.

"No need to beg," he promised her. His body responded for him, moving closer so that he could set the tip of his cock at her entrance. Meanwhile, Lorenzo and Trent took care of desensitizing her, touching her everywhere and kissing her shoulders, neck, and breasts.

All Owen had to do was fuck and they would make sure it was good for her.

He had one job. He could do that.

Owen pressed forward, tunneling within her hot hold. The slick velvet of her pussy welcomed him and guaranteed he wouldn't be able to hang on anywhere near as long as Lorenzo had before he needed to call in reinforcements.

Fortunately, now that she'd already come twice, Holly seemed in the rhythm of things. It didn't take many pumps for her thighs to start trembling around his hips.

"Damn," she moaned. "You're so good at that. Fuck me faster, Owen. Harder."

It *was* what he was best at. Trent was debonair, Lorenzo was sultry, and Owen...well...he was raw and rough around the edges. If that's what she needed, intensity without a lot of polish, she'd come to the right man.

He planted his hands on either side of her and bit her lower lip, claiming her attention. It meant he wouldn't last very long, but that wasn't what she seemed to crave anyway. Not after the slow ride Lorenzo had taken her for.

She strained against him, her body taut and seeking. Rocking, she slapped her pelvis against his, grinding her clit against the base of his dick. She used him, and he loved every moment of pleasuring her. It gave him purpose and made him feel...valuable. Like he was contributing something to their group.

For so long it had been him against the world, he hadn't realized he needed to be part of something greater than only his own self-preservation. Now he knew better.

It was that thought that allowed him to keep plowing into her with the speed and efficiency of a machine, making her shudder and cry out his name, over and over until she began to tremor.

Holly gripped his forearms and dug her nails in, only spurring him on.

She was the most beautiful thing he'd ever seen, the most amazing woman he'd known, never mind slept with. He wished he could have told her all that, but it was too difficult for him. So he tried to translate his emotions into movement, and hoped she understood what their bodies were saying when they came together so perfectly.

Almost too perfectly.

Owen clenched his jaw as Holly began to chant his name, and prayed he could hang on a little longer, because they were about to take things to the next level.

7

———

Lorenzo saw Owen's hips jerk and knew the man was close. When Holly screamed and bucked, Owen froze. He threw his head back and swore at the ceiling, but by some miracle, despite having his cock massaged by Holly's tight pussy, he didn't come with her.

When she'd settled, Owen withdrew, his cock painfully hard and darker than Lorenzo had ever seen it before.

So why had he held off? For the same reason they all had, Lorenzo figured.

They wanted to do this together. It didn't seem right to finish this any other way than how they meant to go forward. As one unit.

Holly had rolled onto her side, melting over Trent's chest, her head lolling on his shoulder as Owen cradled her, caressing her and whispering over and over how beautiful and brave she was, how magnificent.

And when Trent said, "One more time, Holly. And this time we want to let go when you do."

She moaned but didn't object or say she didn't have it in her, because they all knew she did. Holly blinked her eyes open and smiled softly. "Yes, I want that too. But how?"

Her genuine curiosity made Lorenzo's cock twitch. He couldn't wait to show her the variety of ways they could make love to her and discover more than he already knew himself.

"Let us worry about that." Trent kissed her neck, making her sigh and squirm despite her recent releases. "All you have to do is be open to us."

Holly closed her eyes again and went lax, trusting them completely.

Lorenzo groaned when a bead of slickness spilled from his tip and rolled down his knuckles. He hadn't meant to touch himself, but by the time he realized he had, he was fully hard again, ready to give Holly as much of him as she could take.

Trent looked at him and nodded. "I know. Me too."

Then he rolled Holly over so that she was lying on her stomach, her arms at her sides and her legs spread slightly. Trent kept kissing her neck, inspiring her sighs, while his hips began to move, stroking himself through the cleft of her ass.

Owen groaned as he realized what Trent had in mind. If he fucked her there, one of them could fill her pussy at the same time. And the other, well... there were options.

But no matter what, they were going to be inside her together.

No one left behind. No one left alone.

That revelation turned him on so much, there was no way he could stay apart any longer. Lorenzo went down beside them, his thigh touching Trent's and his cock pressed against Holly's hip. She must have felt the heat and weight of it because she moaned even before he started humping against her in time to Trent's motions.

He would have looked to Owen and told him to join them, but when Lorenzo glanced over, he already was. The three of them rubbed themselves against Holly's smooth skin, content to feel her close to them, until she whimpered and lifted her ass.

"You need more?" Trent asked, taking her cheeks in hand and spreading her so that on his next glide, the head of his cock nudged her tight hole.

Holly gasped but nodded, then cried, "Please!"

Trent tortured them all by being his usual, thorough self. He dipped his cock lower and plunged it in Holly's drenched pussy, just once, before returning to her ass. He dipped his fingers inside her and slathered them before pressing one to her asshole. Her own natural lubrication eased the way as Trent rubbed around his finger with his opposite thumb.

Every time Holly relaxed, he advanced deeper until she was taking him effortlessly.

Lorenzo and Owen kept stroking themselves against her, keeping their cocks ready for wherever she could use them. Because it was going to be soon, and it wasn't going to last forever. But it was going to be intense if they did this right.

Lorenzo felt like every foursome they'd ever had before had taught them what they needed to know in order to give Holly the maximum amount of bliss.

"Oh!" she cried out, though more in surprise than anything that sounded like discomfort.

"You okay?" Lorenzo asked as her fingers curled in the sheets. He reached into the drawer of the bedside table and grabbed a bottle of lube. There was no doubt now where they were headed. So he drizzled it over her hole and Trent's hand, making sure there was plenty to go around.

"So good," she breathed. "I never... Didn't expect..."

Lorenzo couldn't help but kiss the side of her face then. "None of us imagined it could be like this. But I'm glad this is where we ended up and that we found each other."

Owen grunted his agreement as he nudged Holly's opposite hip with his cock.

"You ready for Trent, *coração*?" Lorenzo nuzzled her shoulder. "He's dying to be inside you."

"I think so." A hint of trepidation in her voice made him clasp her hand.

"You can take it," he promised her. "Let him in."

Holly stilled and her back unknotted beneath his and Owen's caresses. Unable to resist any longer, Trent withdrew his fingers and replaced them with the tip of his hard-on. Watching the blunt head disappear into Holly's ass as they both groaned and stiffened only made Lorenzo harder.

Knowing that two of the people he was closest to in the world were experiencing so much joy impacted him too. "That's right, Holly. He's going to make it so good for you. For us all."

She shuddered at that before planting her knees in the mattress and angling her pelvis to make Trent's invasion more effective. Owen took the opportunity to slip his hand beneath her and give her something to grind on as he rubbed her clit.

"More" she gasped. "Fill me."

"You've got all of me," Trent promised before nipping at the back of her neck.

"Not you. Them." Holly seemed beyond full sentences. And Lorenzo could relate. He stopped thinking for the first time in forever and simply did what felt right. It was liberating and dangerous, because some of the inhibitions he had kept him from sharing too much—like his heart—and getting hurt again.

He was willing to risk it. Just this once. To show her what things could be like if they were all as brave as she was.

Trent looked at Lorenzo and said, "Give her what she needs."

Then he wrapped her in a bear hug and rolled to his back, letting Holly blanket him, this time impaled on his cock. Her legs draped over his spread knees, leaving her pussy open and welcoming for...someone.

Lorenzo looked to Owen, who said, "You go. I'm still too close to the edge for that."

He nodded, not needing to be told twice. Lorenzo crawled into place, his cock naturally aligning with her body. It shocked him when Owen reached out and nudged him, encouraging him to press inside with a rasped, "What are you waiting for?"

Though Lorenzo would have liked to stretch things out all night, he knew they'd pushed their luck already. Holly shot him a wobbly smile, then grabbed for his hips, drawing him to her, impaling herself on his shaft. She was slick yet tight and so damn hot she nearly scorched him.

As his cock slid along the ridge of Trent's, which he could feel through the delicate tissues of her body, the other man drummed his heels on the bed.

Owen stared at Holly, making sure she was okay as Lorenzo stretched her around his cock. As he'd promised her, she had no trouble taking them both. Instead she cooed, her toes curling as she rocked toward him, rather than away.

"So full," she gasped. "So good."

At the same time her hand reached out for Owen, her fingers curling around his shaft. She pumped him, making him hiss.

"You know what he likes?" Lorenzo asked Holly, determined to prove how perfect she was for them. Trent groaned from beneath them, and his cock slipped across Lorenzo's, separated only by a bit of Holly.

Holly licked her lips, and Lorenzo chuckled. "Yeah, what guy doesn't? But even more...he's obsessed with your tits."

She blinked up at Lorenzo and then Owen as if trying to clear her mind long enough to see if what he said was true. Lorenzo didn't want her to think that hard. He wanted her to ride the feelings and emotions coursing between them, like he was. It was the only way to protect himself.

So he yanked Owen's arm.

The man only had two choices: throw his leg over Holly and straddle her in front of Lorenzo, or squash her. And they both knew he would never risk injuring her.

Over Owen's shoulder, Lorenzo witnessed Holly's shocked expression morph into a smile. Her eyes sparkled as she put her hands up and cupped her breasts, mounding them together. Lorenzo did what he could to facilitate things by running his hands beneath his balls and collecting the slickness there before reaching around Owen and painting her own arousal and the extra lube he'd poured on her between her breasts.

She was so wet, her chest glistened, and he had to admit his cock jerked at the sight.

Owen, however, was a goner. He used two fingers to press his dick down and aimed the head at her cleavage. Holly shaped herself around Owen's cock as it poked between the pillow of her breasts and protruded from the other side.

Holly lowered her chin and opened her mouth, taking what she could reach of his tip between her lips. Damn, that had to feel incredible.

Trent stared at the show they were putting on over Holly's shoulder, moaning as he ground up into her ass from below. Lorenzo couldn't help himself either—he began to move, pressing into her before retreating, just enough to do it again.

He and Owen bumped into each other somewhat awkwardly as they fucked her pussy and chest, so Lorenzo thought *fuck it* and put his arm around Owen's waist, locking them together.

The other guy shot him a what-the-hell-are-you-doing stare before he realized how good it would feel as Lorenzo fucked forward and the resulting motion forced Owen's cock between Holly's breasts. It only took two strokes before Owen relaxed and let Lorenzo drive them both.

Teamed up to provide Holly with as much pleasure as possible, it also guaranteed their own enjoyment. Trent cursed then matched the rhythm Lorenzo set, pumping into Holly's ass as he retreated. They passed each other with every stroke, only enhancing each other's efforts.

Holly's hands gripped herself harder, her fingers pressing on her nipples as the three of them made love to every part of her they could. For Lorenzo, that included her mind and her heart.

Trent whispered sweet encouragement to her as Owen cupped the back of her head and lifted it so that he could feed her more of his length. Lorenzo picked up the pace, sensing the energy crackling between them and the escalating desire that would soon rain euphoria on them all.

He wanted that for them.

Not only for one night, but for the rest of their lives.

Some people might say it was too soon to know that's what the stakes were in this exchange, but he could honestly say none of their previous experiences had ever been like this. This was who they were meant to be and he wanted Holly—and Trent and Owen—to see it too.

So he fucked faster, and Trent matched him by default, keeping pace as they tunneled deeper and harder into Holly's body.

Her eyelids fluttered and her eyes began to roll back before she scrunched them closed and shouted. "Yes! Fuck yes! I'm going to come. On all of you. With all of you."

"Good girl," Trent murmured in her ear. "Do it. We'll follow you. Now and forever."

Lorenzo wasn't sure she heard him, but his friend's promise struck a lightning bolt of ecstasy and hope straight to his soul. He roared, and Owen shook in his hold. He kept the other man upright as he caved just a split second before the rest of them.

When the first spurt of Owen's release touched Holly's lower lip, she exploded, wringing Lorenzo and Trent's dick with the force of her orgasm.

Lorenzo's chest slapped against Owen's back as he unloaded deep within Holly, flooding her pussy even as Trent pumped his own seed into her ass. The three of them groaned and called her name over and over. If his best friends were even half as entranced by her and what she could do to them, they were mindless with pleasure.

Holly kept coming, her flesh milking him until he was dry. Even still he pumped into her with short erratic strokes as she peaked and began to come back down.

He rode through the climax, dragging every last bit of ecstasy from it before his arm fell away from Owen and he sat back on his haunches, his cock falling from Holly's body.

After they caught their breath some, he had to move or risk crushing them all.

Lorenzo would have damned his liquefied muscles, except watching a trickle of his fluid slip from her pussy and decorate her flesh made him moan instead. She had to know that she belonged to them now, and that they were hers too.

Didn't she?

Instead of slowing, his heart rate tripled, damn near causing the thing to burst in his chest.

Yesterday, this had been the point at which she'd walked out on them. Had they done a better job today of showing her how much they prized her and how desperately they wanted her in their lives?

Lorenzo glared at Trent, insisting without words that the man make things right.

If he fucked up again, Lorenzo would never forgive him. How could he when he knew they'd never find another woman like Holly in their entire lifetime?

8

"Holly..." Trent swallowed hard, and all three of the people in bed with him swung laser-focused gazes at him.

Lorenzo tensed, terrified that his best friend might do something to jeopardize the best thing he'd found in a long time. If Holly ran again, Lorenzo wasn't sure he could take it.

He could lose his best friends and the woman they were falling for in a single heartbeat.

His stomach cramped as he remembered everyone staring at him, while he stood in a tux at the front of a historic church in his hometown, thousands of miles away. The guests had seen his heart shatter when his bride-to-be had left him at that altar, because of a wild night that hadn't been anywhere near as intense as this one.

And now, for the first time since, he was afraid someone else had the power to wound him like that again.

Trent rolled over so that he was looking down into

63

Holly's eyes as he caressed her cheek. "I'm so sorry for not having the guts to tell you this sooner, but..."

Her gaze flicked to Owen and then Lorenzo when Trent hesitated. Lorenzo flashed her what he hoped was a reassuring smile, though it felt kind of wobbly.

When she looked back to Trent, he admitted in a rush, "I love you. I think I probably was halfway there back in college, to be honest, but these past few weeks, they've been so much more than I could have hoped for. You're the perfect partner for me, in all the areas of my life. Please, stay. And not for the money. In fact, I—uh—"

Trent looked over his shoulder at them as if asking how he was doing. Owen nodded.

"You should tell her," Lorenzo confirmed.

"I've already deposited five million dollars into your bank account. It's yours. No matter what you decide to do, with us or while working for *our* company, I never want cash—or the ability to provide for your mom—to be a factor in your decisions." Trent's face flushed then. "If you choose to stay, you're staying for us. And for love."

"And orgasms," Owen chimed in when Holly didn't answer right away. "We have plenty of those left in stock."

Her silence stretched long enough that Lorenzo was sure they'd fucked up again.

"You did what?" she asked, her head canting slightly to the side.

"Uh oh," Owen muttered.

Holly nudged Trent's shoulder. Not quite a shove, but enough that he plopped to his ass on the bed beside her. She reached for the sheet and pulled it up to her collarbones.

Lorenzo was relieved that at least she didn't start getting dressed, or flee like she had before. Hardly able to breathe, he stood frozen in place. His whole body flashed cold as he waited for her to speak.

"Are you joking?" she asked Trent.

He shook his head. "You deserve it. You've helped me so much already. I wouldn't have anything without you. Besides, I care for you and your mom. It's only right. And I want to be sure you're staying because…"

Trent took a deep breath, then said, "Because you love me too. If you do. I mean, if you could in time."

Lorenzo was freaking out for all of them now. Because as much as he was scared of being abandoned, Trent was terrified of being unlovable, and Owen had never had someone he could rely on. If Holly lashed out now, she could cause irreparable harm.

Instead, she opened her arms and flung herself at Trent, taking them both to the mattress. She dusted kisses over his cheeks and mouth while Owen and Lorenzo cracked up. Every bit of Lorenzo's paralyzing fear melted, thawing his heart along with it.

He joined Holly and Trent, with Owen piling on.

Even Moose barked in the background at their antics.

And when they fell into a heap, out of breath, Holly rose to her knees and took turns kissing each of them. Lorenzo tried to show her with every brush of his lips over hers how glad he was to know they were finally in sync.

What they were doing wasn't for money, or even for pleasure. It was for love.

And if she could care for Trent now, maybe she could feel as deeply for him and for Owen as she did for a guy she'd met while in college, a few years down the road. They'd have to take it one step at a time, but at least they'd be traveling in the same direction from then on.

9

Holly hugged Trent. She rested her head on his shoulder as he rubbed her back then squeezed her before stepping away. "I promise I'll come home as soon as I can."

He'd been summoned to the police station to answer some additional questions the detectives had about his father's death, Trent's inheritance, and how that had all gone down. Ford, Brady, and Josh were working some important cases back east, but at least one of them would be joining via video chat as Trent's official legal counsel.

It was serious shit. Indirectly, he'd been attacked through her. Although she'd been the one stuffed in a trunk, he'd been the target of her kidnapping and the subsequent blackmail attempt. They weren't in the clear yet, and maybe never would be again. Trent was right: money brought along a ton of pitfalls she'd never considered. The more money, the more issues.

Things had been hard before. Now they were complicated.

"Do that." She smiled up at him with a measure of

false bravado, afraid to make him think she didn't want him nearby but also needing to be sure he understood that she wasn't the sort of woman who was too clingy either. "Until then, I'll be okay."

"You're sure?" He tucked a strand of hair behind her ear, caressing her cheek in the process.

"I promise." She smiled up at him, then reached out to her sides without looking. As she expected, Lorenzo and Owen were there to grasp her hands. Their steadying holds made her feel stronger, like she didn't have to lie to Trent just to make him feel better, although she probably would have if necessary. "Besides, I've got your roommates to keep me company until then."

Trent exchanged glances with his best friends. She didn't hold it against him that he was so blatantly tasking them with keeping her safe. Not given the circumstances anyway. Ordinarily, she was plenty capable of doing that for herself.

She'd be lying if she said she didn't appreciate their presence and the extra layer of protection given that her captors were still on the loose.

"Okay." Trent leaned in and stole one last, lingering kiss before he sighed and headed for the door. "I'll text you if I can. When she wakes up, tell your mom I hope she's feeling better and that...I'm sorry."

Holly's heart cramped at that. Both that Trent felt guilty for what had happened, and also that her poor mom had spent the day after her surgery sedated and alone because Holly had been too stubborn to let someone walk her home after her argument with Trent.

No more of that dumb shit. They were going to have to face their issues head on if they had any chance of figuring out how to build a relationship that would last.

After the past two nights, the endless reflecting she'd done while stuffed in that godforsaken trunk, and the coming together they'd shared before and after, she was certain that's what she wanted.

"I'll tell her, but I already know she's going to say there's nothing to forgive. Now me, well...she'll probably ground me until I'm forty-two." All three guys laughed. "Go on."

Holly shooed him out the door, then peeked through the sidelight to watch him get in a car with one of the security team—she thought she'd heard someone call him JRad—and pull away from the curb.

"Come on. Let me make you some breakfast." Lorenzo led her into the kitchen. While he busied himself getting eggs from the fridge, she toasted bread, and Owen doled out Moose's kibble. It felt nice to fit in, to be part of a team instead of the sole person responsible for everything. Holly hated to admit it, but she'd been exhausted, and hadn't even realized how badly.

Things were easy here, with the guys, even if they were complex.

They didn't talk too much as they refueled, each lost in their own thoughts. But when she rose to put her plate in the dishwasher even as Owen scrubbed the pan and Lorenzo put the condiments back in the fridge, Owen asked, "You want to go see your mom?"

"Can I?" Holly had assumed the hospital was off limits while she was on lockdown. Hearing her mother's voice would be so much better if it wasn't on the phone call she'd been planning to make a moment after the transplant ward opened and in person instead.

"If you'll agree to take us with you, I'll check with the super cop outside." Lorenzo jerked his thumb over his shoulder to where "not-agent" Lucas had taken up his post and refused to come inside. He was intense.

"Deal." Holly grinned.

A few minutes later, Lorenzo came back inside and pointed to himself while he shook his hips in a way that made it kind of difficult to concentrate on what he was saying. "Who's your favorite boyfriend?"

"Seriously? We can go?" She jogged over and flung her arms around him, laying a kiss on his lush lips. She had to rise onto her tiptoes to do it and his wide shoulders made sure her arms didn't overlap much across his back. With him and Owen, she'd feel secure enough. "Thank you."

"Damn, if I'd known it would get me a hug like that, I'd have braved the super-cop myself." Owen's wry smile still held a hint of uncertainty.

So she pried herself from Lorenzo's grip, which had encircled her waist, and turned to Owen. "You don't have to do anything to earn my affection. You already have it, you know?"

He didn't respond, but she didn't wait for an answer either. Holly smothered him with a tight embrace, then laid a loud, smacking kiss on his lips.

"Now, I'm going to get dressed. I need some concealer and a long-sleeved shirt. Maybe that will be enough to fool my mom into thinking everything is fine."

"Don't count on it." Lorenzo grumbled.

"Yeah, not likely, but...gotta try." Holly winced as she headed for her room and pulled on fresh clothes, then spiffed herself up as well as she could. Not too much, because that would be obvious. But at least she braided her hair and slapped on some lip gloss.

When she emerged, the guys had also changed and

milled around near the door. Owen looked up, his gaze hanging on her.

"What?" She glanced down at herself.

"Just wishing Lorenzo hadn't been so persuasive when he talked to our babysitters." Owen turned away from her as if ashamed to let her see how much he wanted her.

"The doctor already warned us before surgery that her visiting hours would be limited during recovery. If we go now, we'll be home soon enough." She winked at him as she put on her shoes.

Owen laughed, but she had been serious. Would he want to do something about the desire smoldering between them? Or would he insist on waiting for Trent? She looked to Lorenzo, who frowned, then shrugged.

But she couldn't worry about it then, because she really needed to see her mom and follow up with the doctors. Sure, she'd called for updates several times over the past twelve hours since she'd returned, but it wasn't the same as seeing her mother, hugging her, and getting her ass chewed out to make her sure the woman was okay.

"Let's go." Owen opened the door, then stepped cautiously outside.

Lucas relaxed his bulldog stance and said, "There's a taxi waiting at the curb. I'm going to follow you in our van with all our equipment and stay right outside the hospital entrance. Maybe whoever nabbed Holly will be dumb enough to try it again. If they do, don't worry. We've got you."

He pressed plastic fobs that looked like garage door openers into their hands.

"A panic button?" Holly wished she'd had one of those the other day.

Lucas nodded. "Push it if you suspect anything, however tiny, is off."

"I will." There was no way in hell she was getting separated from Owen and Lorenzo again. She wasn't foolish enough to assume she'd be manage to escape twice.

"Go ahead. I'll be right behind you." Lucas strode to his van with only the barest of detectable limps and climbed inside as Owen and Lorenzo sandwiched her in the taxi.

On the way, Owen made small talk with the driver while Lorenzo brushed his thumb over her hand. And when they arrived, Owen paid the man, telling him to keep the change.

"That was nice of you," she said to him when they were heading for the hospital's revolving door.

"Yeah, well, I know what how it is to depend on tips. Some people gotta make up for the rest, you know?"

Holly nodded. Owen wasn't wealthy like Trent, far from it. She suspected his struggles made hers look tame, and yet he was more generous than people who had a hundred times as much. As if he could read her mind, he reopened his wallet, which he still had in hand.

Focused on seeing her mom and getting an update on her condition, Holly didn't notice the man curled up on the bench beside the door until Owen stopped short, and she nearly collided with him.

He fished out a few bucks and tucked them into the Styrofoam cup clutched in the sleeping man's hand. The guy wasn't awake to ask for money, but Owen gave it to him anyway.

Her heart twitched.

Lorenzo paused, holding the door open, and smiled

sadly when he saw what his friend had done. She was going to have to ask what was up with that. Later. After they'd made sure her mom was okay.

Entering the hospital took her breath away, and not because of the astringent odor lingering in the air, stinging her lungs yet somehow failing to make her feel clean. Everything that had happened in the past few weeks felt like a bizarre dream. One she was afraid to wake from, where her mom got the kidney she'd so desperately needed, and Holly had found something equally as valuable in the form of not only one but three life partners.

Things were so different—this future had been inconceivable to her. But now that she had stepped into this world, she would fight to keep from slipping back into her old existence.

They were quiet as they rode the elevator up to the transplant ward. Holly gripped Owen and Lorenzo's hands tighter as they approached her mother's room, afraid of what they might find within it. As soon as she poked her head inside, her mother wagged her finger and shrieked, "Holly Hendricks, what the hell did you get yourself into?"

Holly burst out laughing. She rushed to her mom and tried to ignore the tubes and machines so they could hug each other. "I'm so glad you're okay."

"I could say the same." Her mom glowered. "Don't go scaring me like that ever again."

"Sorry. Believe me, I didn't intend to." Holly wasn't sure how much her mother had been told, but she didn't want to worry her with the full story if she didn't have to.

"I will admit, waking up to find you missing was one way to take my mind off the surgery." Mom lost a bit of her energy then, so Holly helped her to lie back. "When I'm more with it, you'll tell me every last detail. I mean it."

"Yes, Mom." Holly's eyes filled with tears. They weren't entirely out of the woods yet, but this was progress. "You look good. Your color is so much better already."

"I feel ten years younger." Her mom smiled and squeezed her hand. "Thank you for everything you've done for me. It's because of you that I made it this far and that I had this chance at all. You and your boyfriend, of course. I owe you both more than I could ever repay."

Holly's weepiness only increased at the mention of him. She sniffled and so did her mom, who didn't know the half of what he'd done for them yet.

"Where *is* Trent?" her mother asked, her eyes narrowing as if she could spy the answers to her question, and those she hadn't yet probed about, in Holly's expression.

"The police needed to speak with him." She sighed.

"So he's not off licking his wounds because he thinks he got you in trouble or some dumb male crap like that?" Mom was going to be back to her old self in no time at all.

Holly snorted. "Nah, we're past that stage. That was yesterday's drama."

Owen and Lorenzo chuckled in the background, making her grin even as her cheeks heated.

"Good." Her mother huffed. "He's too good for you to let him screw it up."

"You think so?" Holly glanced down at her mom's hand and the tubes pumping medicine into her bruised skin. They were each damaged in some way. Could it be possible that she and Trent could heal each other? Or for that matter, that she could do the same for Owen and Lorenzo?

Her mother had no idea how tricky and delicate things were at the moment.

"I told you to chase him down after dinner the other night, didn't I?"

"Yeah. That feels like three years ago." Holly suddenly felt drained. Owen slid the chair from the window near to her and she sank onto it with a small smile over her shoulder at him.

"An awful lot has happened since then." Mom beamed up at Owen and Lorenzo before reaching out to lift Holly's chin. "Daughter, I know you better than anyone. Or at least I used to..."

She cleared her throat. Lorenzo poured some water from the bedside table into a paper cup and passed it over. Holly helped her mom guide it to her lips to drink.

When she'd finished, she said, "Things are changing for us both. For the better. I'm not saying I'm an expert on stuff like this, but I want you to know that I love you unconditionally, no matter where we go from here or who ends up walking by your side. Whether that's Trent, or someone else, or more than only him... So long as you're happy and treated right, I support you. You know that, right?"

At that, Holly turned to check out the guys' reaction to Mom's approval. Lorenzo had his hand on Owen's shoulder, gripping hard. Owen was frozen, as if he might crumble if he so much as breathed.

"I do, but it's nice to hear it anyway." Holly felt lighter than she had in...well, years.

Lorenzo spoke up then. "No one knows what the future will bring, but I can promise you this: I respect your daughter and I plan to do my best to take care of her for as long as she'll let me."

"Me too," Owen choked out.

Mom stared at them both, but Lorenzo didn't so much as shift where he stood. Finally, she nodded slightly. "Perfect. I'm not going to be around for a while. I'm glad to know she has someone to lean on when I'm not there."

"I thought I was coming here today to make *you* feel better," Holly figured her mother would always one-up her when it came to that. That's what moms like hers did best.

She was damn lucky.

"I do feel better. Much." Her mom sighed. "I think I might even be able to take a proper nap now, if you don't mind."

Holly wasn't really ready to go, but she didn't want to inhibit her mom's healing any more than she already had by stressing her out the day before. "Okay. I'll come back as soon as I'm allowed."

"Good." Her mom peeked at Owen from below drooping lids. "You can breathe. It's okay."

"Sorry. I'm not used to this." Owen unclenched his hand, which had fisted in his jeans, finger by finger. "Talking about feelings and...having someone accept you no matter what."

"Well, you better get used to it, son. I appreciate you looking out for my daughter, but you're safe with her too. With us." Holly's mom grinned. "And you'd prepare yourself for when I'm out of this damn bed. Because I'm a hugger, too."

He blinked, looking so startled that Lorenzo and Holly couldn't swallow their laughter. She imagined her mom cossetting Owen and smothering him in affection until he relaxed enough to let her see the man Holly had gotten glimpses of in the past month of living with him.

"I've got you covered, Mom." She rose and flung her arms around Owen, holding him tight. Quiet and steady, he'd always projected an illusion of calm strength. Who could have known he didn't understand how to show any other part of himself? From now on, Holly was going to make it her mission to teach him how. And to be worthy of his trust.

"That's my girl. Now, next time you come see me, make sure you bring Trent in case I need to talk some sense into him too." Her mom rolled her eyes. Then she rested her head on her pillow and closed them, a smile still lingering on her face.

"Rest, Mom. And get well."

"I'm going to try my damnedest. This place ain't cheap and they're talking about a rehab facility. I bet I can skip that if I learn to do their exercises or whatever on my own." Mom's smile vanished as the reality of her future care needs sank in.

"No need to rush it." Holly cleared her throat. "I've got you covered. Trent made sure of it, okay?"

"He what?" Her mom blinked a few times.

Holly nodded, "It's true. There's absolutely nothing for you to worry about except healing up. I can't wait for you to go home and start living the life you should have had before."

"Well, that makes two of us. You get started on yours and I'll catch up. I love you more than anything, Holly."

"I love you too, Mom."

"Tell Trent I'm going to cook him an even better celebration dinner when we're on the other side of all this."

"His favorite is *feijoada*," Lorenzo said with a wicked grin.

Owen barked out a laugh. "Uh, no. That's *your* favorite."

Lorenzo shrugged. "He already got one meal and messed it up. My turn."

"I'll let you take turns choosing the menu if you share your mother's recipes with me. We're going to need a bigger table, though." Mom beamed. "Now get out of here and do something fun."

"You heard the lady," Owen murmured with an uncharacteristic easy smile that set Holly on fire. When they finished their goodbyes and got in the elevator, he punched the button for the level that housed the cafeteria.

"The taxi the security guys arranged is meeting us on the ground floor," Lorenzo pressed that one too.

"I know. Mind if we make a quick stop first?" Owen asked them.

"Are you hungry?" Holly squeezed his hand. "My mom has taught me a thing or two. I can cook for us when we get home if you want. I'm still making up for missing a few meals myself."

He grinned at her. "I'll get something to hold us over. But yeah, I'll take you up on that."

Lorenzo linked his fingers with Holly's, then drew her aside when they got off the elevator. He nodded to Owen. "Go ahead. We'll wait for you here."

It wasn't long before he returned with two paper bags. He handed Holly one and kept the other. They piled back into the elevator as she opened it up and found her favorite chips and an apple.

"What'd you get?" she asked as they crossed the lobby and into the afternoon air.

"Nothing." He shrugged, then gave his bag to the man

they'd passed on the way in, who'd woken from his nap. "Lunch is on me, buddy."

"Thanks, man. I'm starving." The guy peeked inside and grinned. "The good stuff even. Not just leftovers. Yes!"

Owen held out his fist and let the man bump it before turning toward her as if people did that kind of stuff every day. No big deal. Lorenzo smiled knowingly at Owen, clearly having guessed his intentions.

Right then, Holly knew she was in trouble. Because it wasn't only Trent she was coming to care for but his best friends too. Sex was great. But this... This was dangerous.

10

———

Holly paced.

Trent still wasn't back, he hadn't texted, and now Lorenzo was about to leave too.

"I'll call off if you want." He came up behind her and rubbed her shoulders.

"There's no need. Owen's here. And so is the new shift outside." She jerked her thumb toward the place where Ransom, Sevan, and Levi were hanging out. "As long as they're going to send someone with you too, go. Have fun and rake in those dollar bills while you show the ladies how studly you are."

Lorenzo cleared his throat. "Does that bother you?"

"That they all see what I'm lucky enough to have?" She snorted. "Hell no. Go. Make 'em jealous as fuck."

He grinned, then kissed her before smacking her ass. "For the record, you're the only one getting any of this. Okay?"

She hadn't been about to ask, even if she had wondered exactly how that worked. Were they in an open relationship? Or was she just lucky enough of a bitch to have three guys to herself? It made her greedy and pretty hypocritical, but she liked the idea that they would be all hers, like the arrangement Andi and Kari had with their guys. They had so much to figure out yet.

"Okay." She smacked his ass right back.

"Don't feel like you need to wait up. I suspect you'll be exhausted by then." He winked and strode out the door, which Owen locked and double-checked behind him.

Holly wilted onto the couch. "Hell, I feel pretty dead already."

Owen turned to her with a frown. "Do you want to take a nap?"

"Yeah, but I doubt I could. And if I fall asleep this late in the evening, I won't be able to go back to bed tonight." She held her hand out to him. Without hesitation, he crossed to her and took it. She used their link to pull him down next her so she could curl up against his side and rest her head on his shoulder.

At first he was stiff, as if surprised or uncertain about how to handle her.

Well, that made two of them. She had even less of a clue, since he'd had plenty of experience with foursomes and she'd had none before theirs. So she went with her gut and put her hand on his abs.

"I'll stay here and watch over you. I swear, no one is going to hurt you again. Not on my watch," he promised.

"I believe you." She smiled up at him then, because she did. "It's just that I'm worried about Trent. He's been gone so long. I hope he's okay."

"He can take care of himself." Owen shrugged. "Believe me, I've seen some shit in my life, and Trent is a survivor. He'll be fine."

Holly bit her lip to keep a million questions from

tumbling out of her mouth and overwhelming him. She considered her next move carefully.

They sat in silence until ringing started in her ears. Owen might be the quiet type, but she'd never been accused of the same. "Want to tell me more about the shit you've seen and why you never felt safe expressing your emotions before?"

"Nah, I'm good." He put his interlocked fingers behind his head as if that was that.

Holly wasn't about to let him get away with it, though, not after she'd been forced to admit so much the past few days. She got to her knees on the couch and straddled him, claiming his full attention.

"Are you really?" She flattened her hands on his chest and felt his heartbeat kicking against her palm. "Or is that a kneejerk reaction?"

"It's a hard habit to break." He met her stare. From just a few inches away she could see every golden fleck in his hazel eyes. "Most people only ask to be polite anyway."

"I'm not most people."

"That's definitely true." He smiled then, the real sort, not the perfunctory kind she'd seen him flash at hospital staff or even the agents outside. That alone told her it was worth harassing him a bit more. So she took a page out of her mom's book and channeled the patented Hendricks tell-me-the-truth stare that had always worked on her.

One of his brows rose in response, and she tried to seem stern instead of laughing. She certainly didn't want him to think she was looking down at his fledgling attempts to tap into the emotions she could sense trapped and swirling within him.

"Tell me, Owen. Please. What are you feeling right now?" She took his hand.

His eyes sparkled and she anticipated his smart-ass remark. "Horny."

"Don't give me that. You're deflecting. Let's have a serious conversation." She started to move off of him, but he was faster, snagging her hand and pressing it to the bulge in his pants.

"Am I lying?"

"No, but that's not the whole truth." She swallowed hard. Unless she had been wrong all along. "At least, I don't think it is. Maybe I'm making a mistake."

Holly backed up, withdrew her fingers from his, and began to climb off his lap.

He put his hand on her hip. "Wait. You're not. This has nothing to do with you and everything to do with me. I'm not used to someone being up in my psyche or giving a shit about what I think."

"Do you think you could get used to it? Because I'm kind of pushy and nosy, and if we're going to be living together—and sleeping together—then it's inevitable that you'll have to trust me too."

"I do." He seemed kind of surprised by that revelation.

"Then answer me, please. I need to know where we stand. Do you think of me as Trent's girlfriend who you sometimes fuck, or as someone you want a relationship with out of bed?" Her throat dried out when he still couldn't seem to find the words to respond.

"Okay, look. I'll go first." Holly figured she had to find the balls to put herself out there if she was asking him to do the same. "I'm worried that what the four of us have going on here won't last if we're not all in it. Not only as fuck buddies but as equal partners. Like Kari and her lawyers or Andi and her guys. They're good examples of how to make something like this work. And *that's* what I want. More than a night or two of fun. I want the forever-and-always variety of relationship with each of you. I know it's going to take time, but yeah...that's what I'm hoping for."

Owen let out an enormous sigh, as if he'd been holding his breath for days. She took that as a good sign, along with the fact that she could feel his erection growing where they were pressed together.

His other hand came up and rested in the small of her back, his fingers sliding into her pockets and flexing on her ass a bit, as if he didn't plan to let her go.

"I'm not sure you know what you're getting into. Trent has issues, sure, but he's still pretty normal. He had a complete family and went to nice schools and..."

"He didn't feel any more accepted than you have." Holly put her hands on Owen's shoulders and began to rub them, hoping to keep him relaxed and open. "I'm not criticizing. I'm just not sure that you see yourself the way I do and I wish you could. I don't know exactly what you've been through, but I'm willing to listen if you ever want to share."

He shrugged, encouraging her to scrub the tension from his muscles again. She would do it as often as required in order to soothe him. Being honest, she hadn't ever known she had this side of her—the caretaker—until her mother got ill. Whether it had always been there or had become a part of her then, when someone she loved needed her to develop it, it was there now. A pillar of her identity. Something that fulfilled her. And if it also helped Owen, then she was glad she'd learned these skills along the way.

"I grew up in a shitty area, with shitty parents, and shitty chances. When I got tired of being a punching bag for the string of boyfriends my mom kept around to have access to meth, I ran. I've been homeless. I've done things I shouldn't have to get by. Sold drugs. Stole stuff and sold that too. Fuck, I even sold myself when I had to." He closed his eyes as if certain she would change the way she looked at him when he admitted it.

Holly slid her hands between him and the couch, hugging him tight instead. She wasn't trying to seduce him, she was trying to be what they both needed. At first he didn't react. Slowly, his arms came up and around her too, embracing her in return.

"Sorry that I'm weird and screwed up," he murmured. "I didn't have a mom like yours. No one taught me how to act toward someone you care about."

"Telling them you give a shit is a start." She rested her forehead on his and smiled. "Thank you. And for the record, I think you either already know how to act deep down or you have good instincts or maybe you've learned more than you think along the way. I saw how kind you were to the taxi driver, and the man at the hospital just today. You also made sure the security team had lunch and helped Kari's guys throw her an incredible engagement party when they were practically strangers to you. You treat Moose like he's a son instead of your dog, and you always let Trent and Lorenzo take what they need before you in bed."

"Oh." His mouth snapped shut. "I guess those things are true. I didn't realize you were paying that much attention to me."

"Well, now you know I have been." She leaned in and kissed him lightly before pulling back again, rubbing the pads of her thumbs over his temples while she cupped his head in her hands.

"I've never felt like this about a woman before," he finally admitted.

"What exactly does that mean?" She didn't want to make assumptions or put words in his mouth.

"I don't know how to explain." He leaned forward and brushed his lips across hers. Instead of the nearly desperate way he normally kissed her, in the heat of the moment while inside her or while watching one of his best friends fucking her, this time was different. He was gentle and almost timid.

Her heart ached for him. She realized then that making love was the only language he had to express himself when it came to relationships. So maybe she should let him tell her in the way he understood. The way that came naturally. And when desire eroded his restraint, maybe then he'd be able to overcome his inhibitions.

"If it's too hard to say what you're feeling, then you can always show me." She didn't know about him, but she felt fluent in the dialect of his body when she glided against him sinuously, and he responded by meeting her halfway, eager to bond them even tighter than they had been before.

Owen had to understand that she desired him, and not only because he was thrown in as a bonus in a package deal. No, it was because something in him called to the part of her that had been forced to keep going despite the unfairness of life and the obstacles that had been tossed in her path. She respected the kind of courage and perseverance it took to survive. He was so much stronger than she'd ever been. That both attracted her and made her long to give him the basic stuff he'd missed out on. Like comfort, and trust, and security. Sweetness and light.

"Can this time be different?" she asked him between sips from his lips.

"How?" He stared down at her breasts, making them both remember what it had been like when he'd pleasured himself between them.

"So far it's been a little like having sex with a stranger." Holly blushed because they were both well aware that she'd gotten off on it.

He laughed at that.

"I mean, you might have done that before, but I never have. It's been a fantasy come to life." Male satisfaction curled up his lips at her confession. "It also feels reckless. I didn't know you as well as I probably should have to be intimate with you at first, but I trust Trent and his judgment in picking friends and partners. And now..."

"I want to get to know you even better." He didn't hesitate about that. "I can say that for sure."

"What if you don't like what you learn?" she asked, almost afraid of the answer. She owed it to him though to be as honest as he was being. "If I'm with Trent and Lorenzo but things don't work out with you and me, what would you do?"

"For my whole life, the only constant has been me. If this doesn't happen for us, if we don't mesh, I'll figure something out. We shouldn't not try just to keep from avoiding some what-if." The more Owen opened up—to her and, she suspected, to himself—the more he seemed to convince them both. "You're right. Up until now, it's been fun, but I'd much rather have something more, something lasting, with you if that's what you want too. I guess I didn't let myself get my hopes up that you could be into me, for me, until right now."

Holly couldn't help but grin at that.

"Oh, shit. What have I done?" Owen reflected it right back at her. "Why do I feel like I just unleashed something I'm never going to be able to regain control of?"

"Do you honestly trust me?" she asked between whisper-kisses.

He swallowed hard and tried to rock to the side in order to flip her beneath him on the couch. She planted her knees and leaned the other direction.

No way. Holly resisted. "Do you?"

He drew a deep breath, then sighed. "Yeah."

"Then let me pamper you. When's the last time someone did that?" She brushed the pad of her thumb over his lower lip.

He shrugged.

"Never, I bet. I want to show you how good it can be to let go."

"I don't know, Holly. That...freaks me out." He groaned. "It probably wouldn't be any good for you. I don't think I can—"

"Exactly why you should do it. With me." She kissed him then, reaching between them to stroke him through his pants. "Trust me like you say you do."

His head fell back on the couch, then he relaxed, maybe for the first time ever around her. "Okay, fine. Do your worst."

A rush of excitement and sensual responsibility flooded her. Power and pride. He gave her that.

And she couldn't wait to see what she could do with it.

11

"Come on." Holly couldn't say where she found the guts to do it, but she stood and held out her hand to Owen. When he took it, she led him from the living room they all shared and into *his* bedroom. It seemed important that he know she was doing this because of him and not because he was lumped in as part of a package deal.

When he hesitated at the threshold, a tendril of doubt rose within her. "Is this okay? Or am I invading your space?"

She glanced around at his room, which could have been featured in a commercial for an anti-hoarder show. She'd previously assumed he was a neat freak, or a minimalist, but now she recognized his sparse décor for what it was: the ability to pick up and go at a moment's notice. A form of armor, protecting him from getting too attached. Maybe it was him Lorenzo should be voting most-likely-to-run.

"You didn't want to make your mark here in case you had to move on, huh?" She looked at him over her shoulder. "It hurts less to disconnect if you don't make it a real home."

"How the hell do you get me when no one else ever has?" That set him in motion again. He strode forward a step and then another, walking her backward until her thighs bumped into his mattress. "You're welcome here anytime. I didn't know you were interested in visiting before."

"Now you do." She spun them, shoving his shoulders so he crashed backward onto the bed and bounced a few times as he stared up at her in shock.

His pupils dilated as she stalked him, crawling onto the mattress so that she could straddle him again. Holly planted her hands on his shoulders. His hands came up, cupping her elbows. If that made him feel like he still had some sort of control over her, she'd allow the illusion, if only for a moment or two longer.

"Since words aren't your thing, I'm going to communicate your way. Hopefully, you get what I'm trying to tell you." Holly sank lower so that she was folded, her knees and hips bent as much as possible so her legs zigzagged and her torso aligned parallel to his. She kissed Owen's jaw, then his chin.

When he shifted, trying to capture her lips with his own, she detoured and sucked on a spot on his neck, just below his ear. Despite his hissed curse, she kept teasing him until he went slack, allowing himself to be completely at her mercy.

Only then did she reward him with a long, slow glide of her mouth on his, consuming the sharp exhalation he made when they finally connected. His body was so hard and lean beneath her, like the street fighter he'd probably been, every ripple of his muscles made it clear that he could overpower her if he chose.

Instead, he let her take the lead. Given what he'd disclosed about his past and the world that had shaped him, that was more valuable than anything he could have said. His confidence in her was priceless. And addictive.

So she did it again and again, until they had gone beyond simple kisses into a full make-out session, their bodies amplifying the contact of their lips and teeth and tongues. And still he lay there, refusing to make a move. It wasn't easy for her either, to take the initiative and put herself out there for him to reject.

Except that every moment he didn't shove her away, she grew bolder. She loved the parts of her he brought out when they were alone like this. It was unexpected and arousing.

Holly had no idea what got into her, but she discovered she liked being in command of both of their desires. She was desperate to prove to him that she could be entrusted with more than just his physical needs. This at least was a start.

She pulled away, staring down at him in wonder. Now that she knew this facet of her existed, somewhere deep down, she wanted to take it for a test drive. With him, she felt comfortable enough to do it. So she leveled her best stern stare at him, then commanded, "Wait here."

"Where are you going?" he asked with a worried expression that was half-amusement and half-pain. "Not far I hope?"

She lunged for the basket of clean clothes tucked neatly into the corner. He was a hell of a lot tidier than Lorenzo. Still, she could see two of the black ties he wore to work at the valet stand poking through the open weave.

Oh yeah, that would do.

Holly might have been sporting an evil grin when she snagged them and twirled around, letting them dangle from one of her fingers.

"Holly..."

"Owen." She took the satiny fabric and draped one length over her neck, letting the ends trail between her breasts.

He licked his lips. Shockingly, he didn't move. Not to evade her touch, and definitely not to assert his innate dominance. He allowed her free rein over his body, and a more vulnerable part of him she was sure he didn't often expose.

As she returned to the bed, she held the other tie above him. The cool material caressed his bare chest for her. His nipples were hard and he arched off the bed, the tendons in his neck standing out in stark relief. Owen flung his hand out, smacking the mattress on either side him. His fingers splayed as if he was clinging to the sheets with everything he had in order to grant her wishes.

"Here, let me help you with that." Holly climbed onto the bed and resumed her position, leaning forward to place light kisses on his parted lips. His cock was a thick ridge between her legs.

She couldn't stop herself from sliding back and forth over him, rubbing her mound along his cock, though he certainly didn't seem to mind. This might just work after all.

Holly smiled down at him. "Thank you."

"I haven't done anything." He practically pouted.

"That's exactly what I'm talking about." She kissed the tip of his nose. "I know it's not easy for you to surrender. And I think if we go too much further, you're going to crack. You're not going to be able to help yourself, and will start taking the lead when we both know switching things up could be mind-blowing. So why don't you let me help you? Help us?"

His brows climbed his forehead. "I thought those were for *me* to use on *you*."

She laughed. "Poor Owen. Not this time."

He levered to his elbows but didn't rise any farther. "You're serious? You want to tie me up?"

"I want to teach you to take." She kneaded his chest through his T-shirt until he relaxed again, lowering himself back to the bed. "You don't think I've seen how you hold back in our sessions? How you wait until everyone else is satisfied before you allow yourself to fall?"

"If you think you're going to get me off before I've done the same for you... No. That's not going to happen." He grimaced. "That's a hard limit for me. If you don't enjoy this too, then there's no point."

And right then she understood. That's how he demonstrated his affection. Maybe even his love. By being generous with his attention and by satisfying his partners, putting their needs above his own, like no one had ever done for him. Until now.

"You can hold out if you really want to." Holly shrugged. "But either way, I'm going to take care of you. I promise you doing it will bring me lots of pleasure."

He blinked up at her as if hearing what she was saying for the first time.

"Really?" He tipped his head.

"Yeah." Holly smiled softly. "So you're going to be good and let me have my way with you, right?"

"Uh, I guess." He grinned. "I'll try my best."

"Do you want a safe word?" Holly asked, entirely serious.

Owen laughed. "Nah. Do anything you like, I can take it."

"Okay, but if you change your mind or this gets too scary, just say so. I'll stop if you want me to." She caressed his cheek. "This is about you, not me."

"I think it's about us both." His insight sent shivers down her spine. Because he was right. If this was going to work, they each needed to grow and learn to open up.

Holly nodded, then pointed toward the head of the bed. "Get up there, take your shirt off, and grab the bars on the headboard."

When he did, it took every bit of her acting skills to pretend like his bare torso didn't make her want to skip straight to their very happy ending. So she concentrated extra hard on her mission.

His bed wasn't anything fancy, a few steel rails that connected unadorned square posts on either side. Basic, black, and utilitarian—it would work just fine. Holly looped the first tie around the painted metal before making a few circuits around Owen's wrist to ensure it was padded.

Once she was satisfied that the edges wouldn't dig into his skin, not even a little, she tied the ends, securing him to the bed. She tugged a bit, hard enough to reassure herself he wasn't going to break free. Not even if she drove him wild, as she hoped to soon.

For the briefest of instants, she recalled what it had been like to be the one in restraints, though at the mercy of people who planned to use her as a weapon instead of delighting her.

"You okay?" Owen asked when she should have been posing that question to him.

It took her a try or two to clear her voice before responding. "Yeah. Just remembered when I was stuck in that trunk…"

Owen used his free arm to wrap around her back and hug her tight. She rested against him for a bit, counting his deep breaths, until the cloud of unease passed. "You're in charge now, Holly. Only you get to say what happens next."

As clever as she'd thought she was being, he was smarter. Though it wasn't easy for him either, he was willing to empower her and keep her from feeling like a victim.

It didn't take anything else for her to regroup. She nodded, then bound his other hand carefully, checking the fit of the material before kissing a meandering path down his neck.

His cock jerked between them, inspiring her to do it again and again until he cursed softly and tugged, finding her knots secure.

"Is that okay?" she murmured near his ear.

"If by okay you mean that it makes me so damn turned on I could end this experiment before you've really begun it? Yup." Owen raised his head, then let it drop to the pillow with a groan.

Holly chuckled against him. Oh yeah, this could be fun. "Then I guess I'd better get going, huh?"

"I want to say yes. So why do I feel like that's only going to make this worse?" Owen flashed her a rueful smile, then nodded. "Do it."

12

"Say please." Holly sat up and tweaked his nipple. Though he wrenched away from her in surprise, he was quick to return. His hard-on made it obvious he hadn't hated her rebuke, either.

"Please." Despite her insistence, he seemed genuine when he begged her to continue, so she did.

Holly took her time, exploring every ridge and valley of his body, from his collarbones to the edges of his pecs. If she spent an inordinate amount of time petting his cut abs, he'd just have to deal with her fawning. The hours he put in at the gym or taking Moose for a jog were apparent in the definition of his muscles and the tan skin hugging each of them.

And when she traced the lines from his hipbones to where they disappeared beneath his very low-riding sweats, she wrapped her fingers in the waistband and lifted them over his cock.

A sheen of perspiration made his brow and upper lip shimmer. She inched the soft fabric beneath his ass and down his legs. Before she'd worked them off his feet, he began kicking them off along with his socks.

Owen planted his feet on the bed, then raised his hips, despite her sitting partially on his quads. He made his dick an offering to her.

Now that was an invitation she planned to accept.

Holly reached out and stroked him. She sank lower until her face was even with his dick, then placed a kiss on the very head of his shaft, trying not to grin when he called her name.

"Yes?" she asked, as innocently as she could, while peeking up at him.

"If you do that…"

"Don't worry, Owen." She smiled. "I've got you. I know what you want and if you let me play, you might just get it. This turns me on too, you know?"

"Oh. Okay then. Go for it."

"Don't mind if I do." She surrounded his cock with her hand and fed it to herself, sucking on him lightly and only gradually taking him farther into her mouth, until he nudged the back of her throat.

"Holly!" The headboard rattled as he shook. But she still had plenty of time to tease him. He had more stamina than that. So she pushed on, lapping at as much of his balls and the base of his shaft as she could while she tortured him.

Until his abdomen rippled in front of her face and his thighs began to tense on either side of her ribs. Only then did she allow him to slide free while licking her lips.

Owen groaned. "So close."

"I thought you wanted to wait for me?" she asked, secretly thrilled that he had.

"I do. But…I'm not a very patient man."

"You'll stay here all damn night if I decide you will." She put her hands on her hips, though she couldn't imagine herself having that much self-control.

No, she needed him inside her, soon. But first she was going to give him a break and even them up a bit. She wanted to explode with him, and make his fantasies come true. But to do that, she needed some help too.

Holly climbed Owen until her knees rested on his pillow, on either side of his head. "Bite me if I'm smothering you."

Owen moaned, but didn't so much as graze her with his teeth as she sat on his face. Instead, he began to eat her out with such skill and intensity that she had to grip the metal bars next to his bound hands and hold on for dear life.

He licked, sucked, and shoved his tongue inside her, but it wasn't quite the right angle for what she craved most, so she turned around and wormed her way into position so he could lick her clit.

Holly sighed and kissed his abdomen as he began to suck on her. When he hit the perfect place, she tipped her head to one side and licked along his shaft.

When he did it again and again, she took him in her mouth and sucked, mimicking his motions.

It felt so good she nearly let herself cave and come on his face. But she didn't want that for them. So she distracted herself by toying with his balls. And when her fingertips glanced the flesh beneath them, dangerously close to his ass, he froze.

A strangled groan ripped between them as he went stiff all over.

Holly rolled off him in a flash, sure that if she so much

as brushed his dick, he was going to lose it. Except he took her distance the wrong way.

"I'm sorry. Shit! I don't know why I did that." He slammed his eyes shut. "It's fine. Keep going."

"You reacted like that because it felt a little too good." Holly proved it to them both by reaching between his legs and doing it again.

Owen cursed. He might have tried to suppress his response, but it was too late to hide things from her now. His cock leaked onto his tight abs as she began to press her finger against his ass.

"Fuck, Holly." Owen thrashed but couldn't get loose. It didn't seem like he really wanted to when he admitted, "I haven't done any of this before. Or not in a minute at least."

She paused. "What are you saying?"

"I don't fuck women by myself. It's too...intimate. And I've certainly never let one be on top before. Never mind... you know."

She fit her finger the barest bit inside him. "That?"

"Uh." He groaned. "Yeah. I think that. Maybe you better do it again, deeper, to make sure that's what I really mean. If it doesn't disgust you."

She didn't care if he was trying artlessly to manipulate her, because she believed him about never allowing anyone else to have him like that, and the fact that he was letting her in was all that mattered. "Nothing about you turns me off, Owen. I'll give you this if that's what you need."

Watching him closely, she advanced within him, or tried. He was tight and dry.

"Holly!" he called, this time with a hint of discomfort.

"Sorry." She stroked him until he was fully hard again. "I've never done this before either. Help me help you."

"There's some lube in my drawer." His voice was hoarse and strained as he admitted it, practically asking her to keep playing with his ass.

She turned around and lunged for his nightstand. When she opened it, she blinked a few times before reaching for something. Not the bottle of silky gel, but an object that looked like a slender black cylinder with a significant bend in the middle.

"What's this?" She held it up for him to see.

"Uh—" He turned his head away from her.

Holly's insides went shimmery and she swore she nearly came on the spot. "It's some kind of toy, right?"

When he didn't respond, she perched beside him on folded legs, then tipped his face back toward her. He still refused to meet her gaze until she stoked his cheek and calmly said, "Tell me what you do with it. If you like it, I want to try it."

"It only works on guys. It's a vibrator. A prostate massager, okay?" He blew out a breath and stared at the ceiling.

"Hell yes, that's okay. I've heard that can feel incredible." She didn't realize she'd started rubbing her pussy until his gaze lasered onto her motions. "Can I use it on you?"

"I don't know, Holly." He shook his head. "That doesn't, like, gross you out? Won't it make things weird?"

"No, it doesn't. And no, it won't." She spread herself so he could see just what he did to her. "Can't you tell how wet you make me?"

"How is that even possible? Fuck, I'll never live this

down if the guys find out." He scrunched his eyes closed. "Please don't tell them. Promise you won't."

"Hang on. I let Trent fuck me in the ass just the other day. None of you seemed to care, unless it was to get amped up over it. And I have a vibrator. Should I be embarrassed about using that too?"

His eyes flew open as he stared at her. "Hell no. I would love to see you do it."

"So what's the difference?" She reached down to stroke his cock, bringing it back to peak steeliness, refusing to let his inhibitions drown out his pleasure.

"You don't fuck people while your same-sex friends are in the room." He looked like he would have flailed his arms if they hadn't been secured to the bed. His head came up and his neck strained. "I don't want them to get the wrong idea. I'm not gay. I don't want them to screw me or anything like that."

"You know it's fine if you do. If you're gay or bi or whatever. And it's also fine to be a straight guy who's into ass play. None of those scenarios change how I feel about you or this." She petted his chest, trying to calm him.

"I mean, yeah. It would be cool if I was, but I'm not. I just...get off on this, okay?" he asked again, though she wasn't sure who he was questioning—her, or himself.

"Very. That's sexy, Owen." Holly picked up the toy again and examined it. "So let me do something about it?"

She leaned in and kissed him, showing him exactly how much the idea turned her on too. Slightly because it was new and taboo, but mostly because it gave her another key to unlock his ecstasy. Okay, no. The biggest factor was that it meant he really did trust her fully. There's no way he'd have gone there with her if he didn't.

"If you're sure it's not going to change how you or the

guys think of me, then yeah, go ahead." He groaned, another drop of precome rolling down the head of his cock.

"Hey." She took his face in her hands and stared straight into his eyes. "No matter what we do here today, I won't rat you out. You know that, right? I don't think you have a single thing to worry about if you choose to share this kink with Lorenzo and Trent, but it's your business to tell them or not. When we're together with them, I won't do this, or even hint at it, unless you ask me to first. And when you're ready, you should buy me a big fat strap-on so I can fuck you while they're fucking me."

"Son of bitch!" Owen's breath was ragged now. "It feels so good. This and sharing... It would be *everything*."

"Then I think you should consider being honest." Holly kissed him one more time before smiling down at him. "And until then...enjoy the fuck out of letting me do this to you when we're alone. Ready?"

"Do it," he ordered. She didn't bother to remind him who was in charge, because they both already understood it was her. If it made him more comfortable, she let him wrap his illusion around him like a security blanket. At least for now. "But, uh, maybe not for long? I'm not going to be able to wait for you."

"Let me worry about that." Holly turned around, flashing her ass at him in the process.

"What are you doing?" he asked tentatively.

"I want to be able to see what I'm doing." She glanced over her shoulder. "But I have to tell you, Owen, this makes me so fucking hot, I'm not going to last either. So I'm going to ride you while I do it. You don't mind, do you?"

She took his cock, thicker and harder than she'd seen it before, and poised it at the entrance to her body.

"You're going to kill me." He growled. "You're every dirty dream I've ever had come to life." He spread his legs out wide, giving her plenty of room to work.

She bit her lip, then smiled, glad he couldn't see her expression. It was a rush, to have someone give her this much leeway, and to know that she was about to use it to blow their mind like he had hers so many times lately.

And then she was sinking onto his cock, filling herself with him, hugging him tight within her as her pussy gloved him. When she sat on him, feeling him as deep within her as she could get, she began to rock, screwing him reverse cowboy style even as she leaned forward a bit.

Holly picked up the massager and coated it with lube before lifting his balls and rubbing it around his ass. Owen made a choking sound that had her checking on him. He thrust up into her from below, lifting her onto her knees. "Don't stop now, Holly. Fuck me."

Whether he meant in the ass or by riding him, it didn't matter, because she did both.

Holly introduced the slim black toy into his body, twisting it a bit like she did with her own vibrator to ease its way into him. It was fascinating watching what it did to him, how it made his sac tighten and his cock pulse at the base. And that was even before she flicked it on.

Then his toes curled and he rattled the bed frame.

"Yes! Hell yes!" he shouted.

Owen was damn near legendary when it came to control in bed. But this new side of him had nearly reached its breaking point. And so had she.

Holly rose and fell over him, moaning when his cock stroked deep within her even as she rubbed her clit on his clean-shaven balls. She clamped around him, her wide-eyes flying to his over her shoulder so she could reassure him just how much she was basking in their connection, his surrender, and the ultimate faith he'd placed in her.

"Holly, please, don't stop," he begged though she knew it was for her sake and not his. "Use me to make yourself feel good. Come on me."

"And you'll join me when I do?" she asked, practically pleading herself.

"Couldn't help it if I tried."

"Don't try." Holly ground herself on him, burying him as deep as he could go in her heat and wetness. "There's no need for one of us to be first. We're in this together. Today and every day from now on."

The sound he made was unintelligible when it came to words, but entirely understandable when it came to feels. He knew she wasn't talking only of orgasms and playtime etiquette.

This was about so much more than their bodies.

He was making her heart shudder too. Neither one of them would be the same after sharing something this powerful.

"Deeper, Holly," he barked.

"That's as far as I can get you in me."

"No." He could hardly talk anymore. "The vibe. Angle it. Toward the front. Push it in. Deeper."

"Oh." Right. It was getting tough to think, even for her.

She did as he requested. There was no doubt she'd done it right when he roared, "Fuck yeah! Right there. Keep it right there and fuck me hard. Now."

Holly couldn't help herself. She bounced on him, channeling the inner porn star she hadn't known she possessed until that moment. It was a good thing he was teetering on the razor's edge of rapture with her because her orgasm caught her completely by surprise.

His cock flared inside her, the ridges growing more defined at the same time she crested.

She screamed his name. "Shoot deep inside me. Right now. Fill me up while I fuck your ass. Show me how much you love this."

What the hell was she saying? It was like the spirit of the world's most talented sex worker had possessed her as her mouth moved on autopilot. Her breasts were heavy as she fucked him and she used her free hand to pinch one of her nipples.

She looked down in time to see Owen's ass clenching around his massager and the base of his cock flexing as he did what she told him to do. An orgasm ripped through her, making her strangle Owen's dick as she absolutely unraveled around him.

It seemed to last forever as she rocked on top of him, eventually falling forward, grabbing his knee to keep upright as she continued to rut on top of him. He met every single one of her motions with one of his own, feeding her as much of himself as he could.

"Holly!" he groaned, getting her attention. "Turn it off. Turn it off!"

Oops. She cut the power, then slid the device from his still-shaking body, making him curse and moan in the process. Only then did she allow his cock to slip from her pussy.

Holly turned around and blanketed him. The rush that consumed her was even better than her climax had been. She began to laugh, then dusted Owen's face with butterfly kisses.

"I just came so hard I think my nuts turned inside out

and that's funny?" He pried one eye open, as if he was preparing himself for some kind of emotional blow.

"No. It's just...exhilarating. Such a rush. I've never felt like that before." She made quick work of untying the knots at his wrists and rubbing the red marks there before smothering him in an enormous hug. "Thank you, Owen. For letting me share that with you. It was... Wow."

As soon as he was able, he rolled over, covering her with his heat and weight. She'd been right to tie him up. He couldn't help himself.

But damn, it had been hot as hell while it lasted.

"It was." He surprised her by kissing her gently instead of trying to prove something unnecessary about his masculinity after what they'd done together. "That was hands down the best sex of my life. You know, without the other guys."

Holly couldn't really argue, though it was hard to compare the things she'd done with him, Lorenzo, and Trent individually. Each of them was different and special on their own. It was a three-way tie, she figured. She reached up and brought Owen's face to hers for a series of kisses that helped them wind down.

Eventually he lay beside her, tucking her against his chest. But she wasn't in the least bit sleepy. There was too much to think about, and too many things for them to resolve before she could rest.

13

———

It took a solid half hour of snuggling before Holly was ready to do more than bask in the effect Owen had on her body and her soul. Neither were they ready to fall asleep, though. No matter how much she'd done to wear him out, she could practically hear him thinking.

"So are you ready to tell me what things you're obsessing about?" Holly asked Owen, trailing the tip of her finger down his chest. "It's not about solo sex. I can promise you that part is fine."

He laughed. "I'm worried I might have created a monster."

She smacked him lightly and joined him, mostly because he might be right. "I can't wait to try out my new skills on Lorenzo and Trent."

"See, a very sexy monster." Owen shifted as though he might derail her with another makeout session, or more. Nope. Not tonight. "They're going to owe me."

"Come on, seriously." Holly figured she would break the ice. "I'll tell you mine if you tell me yours. I'm afraid you guys will get bored of me. There's only one of me and I'm pretty sure you're used to...uh...variety."

"Not going to happen." He squeezed her tight. "I've sampled all the flavors available and I can tell you that you're my favorite by far. I'll never get sick of you—or the way you taste, for that matter."

Owen licked his lips, making her blush.

He cracked up at that. "How can you be shy after what we just did?"

She shrugged. "Sometimes it's hard to let go of stuff. Your turn."

This time he didn't object reflexively. He took a moment to consider her question.

"It sounds dumb, even to me." He stared at the ceiling, idly tracing a swirl pattern down her spine while toying with her hair.

"I won't laugh. Fears usually aren't rational."

"Trent has always been one of us. I mean, I didn't know him when he was growing up rich. Hell, part of me didn't entirely believe it or understand exactly how fucking loaded he was. But now that he's rolling in it, what if he changes? What if he wants more than we can keep up with? Splitting the rent on a bigger house is going to be tough. I'm already maxed out, and I'm not the kind of guy to be comfortable riding someone else's checkbook. Lorenzo can afford more than me, but neither of us has a mansion or twelve in the budget." Owen had obviously spent a lot of time thinking about the possibility, though she didn't think his anxiety was warranted.

It went deeper than this single thing. The possibility of falling short cut him where he was already wounded by his past but it was more than that. She tried to understand his perspective.

"You're afraid of being left behind."

"That's more Lorenzo's take on it. I've seen his light on late at night these past few weeks. He's not sleeping well. He's concerned too." Owen cleared his throat. "I wouldn't blame Trent if he took you and left us behind. Lorenzo would, though. I don't think he'd ever get over it."

"I can understand that. But I don't plan to steal Trent away from you guys."

Owen chuckled. "You're cute when you're naïve, you know?"

She tried not to be offended and to really listen to what he was saying since she knew it was so difficult for him to open up. Holly wrinkled her nose and Owen kissed it.

"We're more worried that Trent will decide to keep you to himself. And yeah, losing Trent would suck too. I don't want to say I think of him like a brother since I've seen too much of him for that, but...we're not just roommates either. Not anymore. We've been through so much shit, and now some pretty amazing stuff too." Owen sighed. "Besides, who would get custody of Moose? I mean, you might not have known it when you rescued his puppy-ass that night, but Moose has saved us too. None of us were really ready to let someone in. Not a person, but how do you resist a big, dumb dog? And once he melted our hearts a little, we were more open to exploring with each other to lean on and keep ourselves from getting too tangled up and crushed until..."

"Until what?" Holly wasn't about to let him clam up then. She kissed his jaw, hoping he knew it was okay to tell her whatever it was.

"Until the right woman came along." He stared into her eyes. "You."

Her jaw dropped, and for a moment she couldn't force anything out of her mouth.

"No matter what happens with Trent or Lorenzo or us as a whole, I need you to know that this means something to me. That *you* mean something to me." Owen cleared his throat. "I think you're perfect for all of us. But if that turns out not to be the case, understand you'll always have me. Or at least, for as long as you want me. I've got your back."

Holly's eyes prickled because she knew what it cost him to stick with someone and to say so, to make himself vulnerable to her in ways that went a hell of a lot deeper than allowing her to tie him to his bed and rock his world. The promise he'd just made her was more meaningful than if he'd dropped the L word. In his experience, loyalty and faithfulness had never existed. But he was willing to offer those things to her even if he didn't think she would return them.

Hopefully, he would come to understand that went both ways.

"You can count on me, Owen," she promised. "I don't know what the future holds for us, but no matter what life throws at us, I'll be here for you, too."

He hugged her tight enough that her ribs protested a little, but she didn't dare tell him that. It might have been Moose who blazed the path forward, but it had been Lorenzo and Trent's friendship that had first opened the door a crack, allowing Owen to see that it could be possible for him to form a lasting bond with another person. To care about someone else more than they cared about themselves.

It had taken years for them to build that connection with him. That he would devote himself to her after only knowing her a short period of time, made her that much more determined never to let him down.

In that moment, she knew that she'd fallen for more than Trent, his dog, prosperity, and a life overflowing with pleasure. Holly had it bad for his best friends too.

Trent knew she slept with them. Was fine with that. But what would he think when he realized he'd be sharing her heart and not only her body?

Holly and Owen stayed up talking so late into the night that it was actually early morning when Lorenzo peeked in at the sound of their voices. "Is this slumber party invite-only?"

"Hell yes," Owen said before adding, "And you're on the guest list."

"Let me take a shower, then I'm in." Lorenzo was already taking his clothes off as he spoke. As incredible as he looked, tall and tan and sleek, Holly wasn't sure she could handle more sex that night. Fortunately, Owen was on the same page.

"I hope by 'in', you mean ready for bed." Owen grimaced. "I don't think I'm up for anything else."

"After all that dancing, and the day we had before I went to work, that actually sounds good." Lorenzo winced. "Besides, the guys outside still haven't heard from Trent and I'm starting to get anxious. I'm probably not good for much either. Sorry, Holly."

"Don't worry, Owen took care of me." She grinned.

"Thanks, man." Lorenzo held his fist out to Owen, who grinned when he bumped it.

"More like she took care of me. I might not get hard again for a month." He yawned.

They snuggled while Lorenzo did his thing. Holly had finally started to drift off when the bed dipped and

Lorenzo burrowed into the spare pillow he'd brought to Owen's bed before looping an arm around her and cuddling up to her back. He was warm, and clean, and smelled like a blend of vanilla and fresh sawn wood. Last time she'd nearly overdosed on sniffing his hair he'd told her the scent was called cumaru.

She felt so comfy, and...loved that guilt swamped her. "I hope Trent is okay."

"He's tougher than he looks." Lorenzo smiled down at her, though the corners of his mouth were pinched. He placed a kiss on her neck and held her tighter.

She smiled sadly. "That's got to be good because he looks pretty damn strong to me."

"Let's get some sleep and hope he's home in the morning." Owen curled his arm, eliminating the gap between her and his chest. "And if not, we'll talk to the security guys about getting an update, okay?"

"If they don't know, then we'll reach out to Ford, assuming he's not already on it," Lorenzo added.

"Good plan." Holly sighed. Despite their reassurances, she was still concerned. She hoped nothing about her kidnapping was coming back to haunt Trent. She'd been so stupid, running like that when she should have stayed and fought for what she wanted.

It was too late to change the past, but she swore to do better in the future, for all their sakes. If Trent or the other guys did something dumb, she'd have to show them they were making a mistake and resist bailing.

With her strategy set out in her mind, it began to quiet enough that she could doze off.

Right before she went under, she had a random thought that just popped out of her mouth. "There's a farmers' market every Saturday that has some cool local art I think you might like. If you take me there on a date, I'll help you pick out some stuff to put on the walls. You know, if you want to make this place more your own, put down some roots..."

Owen hugged her. "Yeah, that sounds nice. And normal. You make me more normal."

Holly wrinkled her nose. "Ew. The worst thing anyone could ever call me is boring."

"Oh, I didn't say that. Get some rest and I'll show you how *exciting* you are in the morning."

Lorenzo chuckled. "I'm down for that."

"Deal. Good night, guys."

"Night." Owen kissed her forehead and never once let her go.

From behind her, Lorenzo happy sighed. He whispered in her ear, "You're so good for us. Thank you."

She fell asleep with a full heart, even if she was still worried about Trent and what was taking so damn long. If the guys were concerned too, they hid it from her, crisscrossing her with their arms as they drifted off together.

Trent slammed the door, then instantly regretted it when he remembered that, unlike him, his roommates had probably gone to bed hours ago. You know, like before it had already started getting light outside and the birds were chirping as if the world hadn't gone to shit in the past forty-eight hours.

Moose was right there to greet Trent, his tail slapping back and forth like windshield wipers on the deluge setting. "Hey, boy. I missed you too. Did you make sure Holly was safe for me? Yes, of course you did. You're my good boy."

He ruffled Moose's ears and the dog stood up, his bear-paws nearly reaching Trent's shoulders as he tried to lick Trent's face.

"You going to make out with the dog all day or get your ass in here and tell us what's going on?" Lorenzo bitched from the direction of Owen's room. Huh. Trent would bet the millions he probably wasn't going to have for much longer that Holly was in there with them.

At least one thing was going right.

"You've never been a morning person, have you?" he teased as he headed for the open door into his friend's room.

Trent figured it said something important that Lorenzo, Holly, and Owen were tangled up together there rather than in Lorenzo's room, where they usually had their foursomes. She was changing them, breaking through walls he hadn't even realized they had. Hell, the women they'd shared before had never actually made it to the sleeping part of using the bed.

Sleepovers weren't their MO. Or they hadn't been before Holly.

"Going to join us?" she asked with a sexy, sleepy smile that made what he had to tell them ten times worse. Even from his place in hell, Trent's father was fucking up Trent's love life. That bastard.

"It'd be better if you came out here so we can talk." He hated himself when she sat bolt upright. The sheet and comforter tumbled to her waist, revealing her pert breasts. "Maybe put some clothes on too."

"Oh shit, this must be serious," Lorenzo tried to joke, but it fell flat because Trent didn't deny it. And just like that, the three of them were rolling from bed and searching for something to wear.

"I'm glad you three had a nicer night than I did." It wasn't sarcasm—it made him feel better to know that they'd been looking out for each other. If the worst came to pass, they might have to do without him for a while. His stomach cramped.

Trent spun away and went into the kitchen to put on a pot of coffee. He was going to need a mug or three to make it through this discussion. Before he'd even finished pouring water into the machine, Holly trotted up behind him and threw her arms around him, making him slosh just a little.

He didn't mind. Standing there, he absorbed her warmth and the comfort it brought to have her wrapped around him, even in such a platonic way. He'd barely recovered from nearly losing her when things had spiraled out of control again.

"You guys sit down. I've got this." Owen nudged them aside and took up where Trent had left off while Lorenzo grabbed a box of leftover donuts they'd picked up for themselves when they'd gotten some for the security team outside the day before.

"Are you okay?" Holly asked, taking Trent's hand as she sat in the chair next to him at their dining room table. "What took so long? We were so worried."

"The cops had a lot of questions." He pinched the bridge of his nose, unsure of where to start. Things had unfolded as he'd sat in the cold, stark interrogation room. And he didn't want to disclose every detail of the gut-wrenching journey he'd been on there to them. This was going to be hard enough without misplaced guilt eating at them. Because, for some reason that he was pretty sure didn't have to do with his inheritance, they actually gave a shit about him.

Lorenzo leaned forward, studying his face. "For you? Why would they be on your ass? They don't suspect you of being involved in Holly's kidnapping, do they? That doesn't even make sense."

"No, I think they know who was behind that bullshit." Trent felt acid burn up his esophagus. Maybe coffee wasn't the right call after all.

"Who?" Owen asked as he joined them, and the gurgling of brewing coffee shattered their tense silence.

"Does the name Joey Bones ring a bell?" he asked Owen, who'd been involved in some shady shit before he'd gotten his life together.

"What the fuck would he have to do with this? He usually does jobs for...." Owen stopped. "Oh. Shit."

"Let me guess." Trent gripped the table. "Rich people who don't want to get their hands dirty. Right?"

Owen nodded.

"What are you trying to get at?" Lorenzo asked.

"Son of bitch." He pounded his fist into his opposite palm. "They think my mother arranged to have Holly stolen from us so she could sell my wife back to me. No, what they really believe is that she was trying to scare me out of collecting my inheritance at all."

"What?" Holly stood up and slapped her hand on the table. "How could she do that to you?"

"To *me*?" After everything that had happened, Holly couldn't possibly be outraged for him and not at him, could she? "You were the one scared, alone, and hurt. Because of me and my tainted money and...mostly, my family. I made excuses for my mom when she let my father kick me out, disowned me, whatever. I figured she didn't have any power compared to him. That she was too hooked on his wealth to live without it. But if this is true, and I'm starting to think it might actually be, then that's it. I've lost not only my father but my mother too. I could never forgive her for doing something like that. It crosses every single line I could draw."

"This isn't a fucking game! It's not a turf war or some bizarre power struggle. Joey Bones doesn't play. And for what? Pure greed?" Owen roared. "That's sick!"

Trent faced them, anguish and embarrassment shredding him apart. "I know. What if Holly had gotten killed? How could someone who was supposed to love me use her like some pawn in a dangerous game? I'm so sorry I got you all involved in my mess. This can't ever happen again. It won't. I swear it."

He gathered Holly into his arms and dragged her onto his lap, burying his face in the silk of her hair. His entire chest ached as if someone had punched him in the heart. His own mother had tried to get to him through the woman he loved. She didn't give a shit about his happiness or that he'd found someone—three of them, really—to spend his life with. All she cared about was hoarding some fraction of his father's total estate, which she didn't even need to live without a care for the rest of her life.

How had he come from them? And how much worse would it be if someone who didn't have any connection to him got a similar idea? He couldn't risk it.

Holly rubbed his back and kissed his collarbone. "It's okay, Trent. You're not to blame for the actions of others. It's time you left them behind. It's okay to let go of a toxic relationship, even if it's one you were born into. *We're* your family now."

And he might be about to disappoint even them. Would they react better than his parents had when he let them down? When he confessed that he couldn't provide what they needed?

"I'm so sorry." He moved Holly back just enough that she could stare straight into his eyes. "Not only did I push you away, but it was my own relatives who assaulted and terrorized you. I don't deserve you and because of them, I might not get a chance to make it up to you either."

"Wait. What?" Owen asked. "What are you saying?"

"As best I figure, this isn't over. And it won't be until I

cut all ties, like Holly just said." Trent gulped in some air and then blurted out the truth. "If I keep this money, I'm radioactive. None of you can be near me safely. And if I have to choose, I would much rather have you than a big fat bank account. I'm going to give it back."

"You can't!" Holly shot to her feet.

Trent stopped breathing. Was that it? Would she leave if she knew he had nothing to give her? Would she reject him like everyone else he'd ever cared about had too?

"I know you stayed with me this past month because of our deal. And the cash." Trent swallowed hard. "I'm sorry I wasted your time."

For a second he thought she might slap him. But Lorenzo was there behind her to clasp her and put his arms around her waist, keeping her in place. His friend should have let her take a swing, he deserved it. For crushing her dreams. And because part of the money was spent.

They weren't going to cut the kidney out of Holly's mom, so at least something good had come from this temporary insanity, where he'd actually believed his dreams—for his company, for the girl next door, and for all his desires—were coming true. He should have known better.

"Before you get too carried away, can I ask if you've spoken to your mom?" Owen asked, too calm for the rage seething in his eyes. There was too much anger, hurt, betrayal, and disappointment zooming around the room for Trent to sort things out on the fly, but he didn't see how any of them were going to come out of this unscathed.

He shook his head. "What's the point?"

Owen shrugged, "Maybe there's some other answer

than something this extreme. And if not...then you can move ahead like you intend to anyway."

"No!" Holly struggled, but Lorenzo settled her with murmurs that Trent couldn't quite make out.

Trent pulled his phone from his pocket and stared at it long enough that Moose came over and put his head on Trent's thigh, his worried gaze shifting between the four masters he had wrapped around his tail.

"Okay, fine." Trent pulled up his contact and used the one for his mother, which he hadn't touched in years. After this, it would be time to delete it for good. But for them, he would try one last time.

"Savannah speaking," came his mother's cold greeting, so different from Holly's mom. There would be no hugs offered, even if they were in the same room. He already knew this was a terrible idea.

"Hello, Mother." Trent gritted his teeth.

"Cut the nonsense," she snipped. "There's only one reason you're calling. And it's not to chit-chat."

Trent hated the part of him that still, after all this time and proof that it wasn't ever going to happen, wished that he had a mom who would value that sort of relationship. Damn it.

Holly put her hand on his forearm and squeezed before he pulled away, her comfort too hard to bear in the face of his mother's disdain.

"No. I was hoping you could be reasonable, for once." Trent slammed his eyes closed, unable to see the pity in his friends' and lover's faces when he asked, "Do you hate me that much? That you would attack your own son over money?"

"You walked away from this life and everything it held for you." His mother's best down-her-nose glare was obvious, even over the phone. "You gave it up for fun and filth, and now you want to eat your cake, too."

"Ironic, coming from you." Trent was wasting his breath, he knew it. "Then again, what would you know about love? About passion for people instead of status and estates?"

"Are you that stupid, Trent? I thought I raised you to be more cunning. This woman you're tangled up with wants your money so bad she's willing to spread her legs not only for you, but to whore herself out for your friends too, and indulge your perversions. What other reason would someone as kind, and sweet, and smart as your lawyers tried to convince me she is, sign up for that sort of life? Who would choose that sick existence when they could have anyone they wanted?"

His mother was right. Holly was way out of his league. For a moment, Trent wondered if she saw things more clearly than him.

His glance flicked to Holly, and she recoiled as if he'd struck her.

The more time he wasted on his family and their fortune, the more she got hurt. That was unacceptable. "You know what? Fuck this. I don't want your money. I'm sending it back, minus five and a half million dollars or so, which I've already spent."

"How the hell did you waste that much money so fast?" his mother shrieked. "I told the police, and I'm sure they told you, that if I don't have every penny back by the end of the day tomorrow, I'm charging you with fraud. Your sham marriage won't stand up in court. Without *my* money, that bitch will be gone before your cell door slams shut. Hell, maybe I'll even pay her to flip on you so you'll wake up once and for all. You can thank me later."

"That's enough!" Holly swiped his phone from his hand and said, "The only thing that could make me leave is if your son listens to your bullshit, you diamond-studded cunt."

Then she hung up with a stab of her finger that put Trent's phone screen at risk of shattering.

Owen and Lorenzo whooped as Trent's stomach knotted itself.

Because he couldn't stop replaying his mother's speech in his mind and wondering...why would Holly want someone like him? He had nothing to offer her anymore and might not even be around to love her for years to come.

"Why the hell do you look like you're actually listening to anything that bitch said?" Holly sliced her hand through the air.

"Because in some ways, my mom was right." Trent could hardly think past the blinding fear and pain she'd planted in his core, reopening festering, never-healed wounds. "Our deal was money for fake marriage, and I might not be able to live up to my end of the bargain. I won't blame you if you hate me."

"Did you just call our relationship fake *again*?" Holly's tone went up several octaves. "Because if so, maybe I don't know you as well as I thought. Or maybe I was right the other night. You don't see us the same way I do at all!"

"Holly, you're mashing each other's buttons." Owen stood, holding his hands out as if trying to stop the disaster unfolding. "Stop and think about this."

"No!" She glared at Owen, who sat back down. "First, he didn't even consult us before making such a monumental decision, to give all that money to his black-hearted mother, who doesn't deserve one penny when he was doing something good with it. So many people were going to benefit from it!"

"Including you?" Trent looked up at her, feeling beaten.

"If you insinuate one more time that I'm some kind of fucking gold digger, I swear, Trent..." She trailed off, her cheeks as red as when they made love to her. But then she stopped and blinked slowly before saying, "Except, I guess I am. I can't give that money back. My mom needs it."

She started to retreat one step and then another, dusting off Lorenzo's arms when he tried to stop her.

"I would never ask you to." Trent stood, holding his hands out to her, but she only backpedaled more, slipping through his fingers. "I understand what it means to you and your family. Let her file charges against me. The cops will probably be able to get the evidence to prove she was behind this and even if she can still sue me, we've got Ford, Brady, and Josh to help if they can put me on a payment plan. If all else fails, a few years of my life are worth sacrificing if it gets you what you need."

"How can I choose between my mom and you? There has to be some other way." Holly went pale.

"There isn't." He'd spent the past fifteen or so hours trying to brainstorm one.

"I won't let you give everything up for me—your vision, your company, hell, your *freedom*. I won't." She kept reversing out of the kitchen and across the entryway until the doorknob jabbed her in the spine. "You're going to change a hell of a lot of lives, like you've already changed mine. But only if you're here to work on your inventions before your competitors do. I'll figure this out somehow. I'm not worth ruining your future for, no one is."

"I'm telling you, you are. That and more." Trent held his hands out toward her.

"To me too." Owen added, looking crushed. "I thought you understood that after last night."

Holly's gaze zinged between him, Owen, and Lorenzo, who was standing as still as a statue, his face frozen in horror as his worst nightmares were coming to life before their eyes. Her lip wobbled as her eyes filled with tears. She shook her head. "I'm sorry. I can't stay."

Owen cursed and rose as if to go after her.

"Let her go." Lorenzo shocked them all, making Trent's insides cramp. "If she's going to bail, she doesn't feel about us like we do about her. It's better to know that now rather than later. Trust me."

His bitterness kicked Trent in the nuts. He'd broken every person he cared for. He didn't deserve any of them. "I'm just glad we had you for a little while."

"I'm not going to stand here and watch her run away from us again. From what we have." Lorenzo shot Holly a look so dead and devoid of the affection he always had for her that it chilled Trent to the bone.

This moment could ruin everything. As if his family hadn't already taken enough, they were going to destroy this too. When would he fucking learn?

15

———

Holly felt sick. The room spun around her and she couldn't make it stop, not with all this new information and the emotions shocking and freezing her as if she'd taken a snowball to the face. Owen's betrayal, Lorenzo's disillusionment, and Trent's solemn acceptance bombarded her. How could she stay in the face of all that?

She just needed some air, space to breathe and think.

Lorenzo slapped his hand on his thigh. "I fucking knew it. Hell, maybe you *were* in it for the money after all."

He paused, staring straight into her eyes long enough that she could have denied it, but she didn't. How could she when it was the truth? At first, all she'd thought about was her saving her mother's life. If she denied that, she'd be lying even if they'd made it about so much more every moment since.

So he turned with a curse and stormed out the back door, letting it bang closed as Moose trotted after, too late to join him. The dog sat there, whimpering in Lorenzo's wake.

Holly knew exactly how he felt.

"How could you do that?" Holly shrieked, her anxiety morphing into rage that she vented in Trent's direction. "How could you listen to your mother? Let her get her way?"

"Holly, it was the only way to keep you safe!" Trent threw up his hands. "Don't argue with me about this."

"I'll argue with you about any damn thing I please." She crossed her arms. Wasn't it only a few hours earlier that she'd convinced herself she could conquer the world if she worked problems out with them instead of bailing?

But that had been when she believed he cared about her opinions, when she thought he would consult her, Lorenzo, and Owen before doing something reckless that could endanger everything he'd worked for. When she believed he'd valued their relationship more than his family's money.

How would he feel if he lost it all because of her?

Owen stalked closer, putting his hands on her shoulders and staring into her eyes. He shook her a little. "Holly, stop this. I trusted you, now you have to do the same for me. You're about to make a mistake that I don't know if we can fix. Sometimes you have to rely on the people who love you to take care of you. Sometimes you can't be the one to make everything okay. Let Trent do this. He's right. We don't need his family's money to be happy, to work for what we want together."

"What if he gets in trouble because of me?" A tear rolled down her cheek and he kissed it away.

"It's his choice." Owen leaned his forehead on hers and she suddenly felt stronger, more grounded. "And besides, we know some kick-ass lawyers. Just because his mom is threatening this bullshit doesn't mean she's going to get away with it. Why don't we at least talk to Ford, Brady, and Josh and see what they can brainstorm? Maybe instead of just the five million Trent gave your mom, he could donate all of it to charity or something. What a classless bitch would his mother look like if she objected to that? Huh? And then there'd be no reason for her to come after you anymore. Maybe there's a way to navigate this clusterfuck that doesn't let her win. Would that be better?"

Instead of reflexive denial, Holly took a deep breath and then another and really thought about what he was saying. Her shoulders dropped and she sagged against him. "Yeah. Okay. All I care about is that Trent doesn't put himself in danger to keep me out of it. That's not a tradeoff I'm willing to accept."

Owen's strong arms were there to wrap around her as he rocked her. "We'll figure out a way. It's going to be okay, Holly. Because I love you. We all do."

Trent rushed over and joined them. He put his arms around her too. "I'm so sorry, Holly. I'm trying to do my best, but I'm obviously fucking up. Owen is saying what I should have. I don't know how he knows the right words but yes. Everything he said."

Owen smacked Trent's chest with the back of his hand before hugging her again. "Tell her. Right now. Say in no uncertain terms that this was *never* about the money."

"It wasn't," Trent said in an instant. "Not between you and me. And if giving it all away proves that, too, then I'm ready to sign the papers. I love you, Holly."

She hiccupped, then clutched both Owen and Trent to her with trembling fingers. "I love you too, both of you.

And I'm so scared of losing you that I can't think straight."

"It's going to be okay. Somehow," Owen promised both her and Trent.

She kissed him and then turned toward Trent, who closed the gap and crushed his mouth to hers. When they finally pulled apart, her head spinning, he sighed. "But first I think you need to convince Lorenzo of that."

Holly winced and buried her face against Trent's shoulder for a few moments. "I really screwed up with him. I almost did the one thing he can't handle. Again."

"We've all messed up. And we will again," Owen told her. "But you can fix it."

Holly stood straighter, womanning up. "I'm going to grovel and hope he'll understand."

"And if that doesn't work, I promise you a blowjob will." Trent's smile emerged from beneath the worry lines marring his handsome face. For that alone it was worth it.

Holly laughed, though it sounded a bit like she was choking. "Got it. Apologize. On my knees if necessary."

Owen shook his head, but he chuckled as he fixed her hair. "Next time we fight, make sure it's me you upset, okay?"

She couldn't help it. She smiled too and wiped her tears. "I'm going to make this right.

"Take your time. And while you're busy blowing Lorenzo's...mind, I'll start making some calls and figuring out the best way to get this done. I'm going to keep you safe, Holly. We'll figure out the rest together, okay?" Trent kissed the side of her face, then let her go, trusting her to take care of what she could while he did his part.

For the first time she realized their strength wasn't in doing everything together, it was in balancing each other out. And until Lorenzo was part of that equation again, things wouldn't add up.

"Okay." She took a deep breath, then crossed the kitchen and living room to the back door. She nudged Moose aside before muttering, "Wish me luck."

"You don't need luck when you have love on your side," Owen told her.

She blew him a kiss, then went out into the yard to do the right thing.

16

<hr>

Holly stood on the threshold, scared of doing what she had to but even more terrified that she wouldn't be able to pull it off. In the background, she heard Owen baiting Trent. "Lorenzo doesn't stand a chance. Ask me how I know. No really, ask me. You're going to be so fucking jealous."

"I knew it. You bastard. I was getting grilled by the cops while you were here doing...whatever it was you were doing. You better tell me every last detail. It's the least you can do."

Their bickering, even if it was for show, did its job. It gave her confidence. Things could go back to normal between them if she handled this right. Holly shut the backdoor quietly behind her, then took a long, deep breath before emerging from the shade of the house and into the sunshine.

For a moment, she tipped her face up into it, letting the first really hot day of the year seep into her bones and lend her strength as her eyes adjusted to the brightness.

Sort of like how she was getting used to the way the three men she loved illuminated the rest of her existence.

There was no doubting it.

The thought of losing them wouldn't make her do and say stupid shit if she didn't care a hell of a lot. Unfortunately, it might be tough to convince Lorenzo of the truth when she'd done the one thing that would prove otherwise to him.

He stood at the edge of the yard, shirtless, chest as bare and raw as his emotions while he stared at the slight ripples crossing the surface of the modest pool in their backyard. It wasn't big but it was pretty, with an irregular shape and a succulent garden border that surrounded it and an entertainment area holding a grill, a table and chairs, and a pergola, which shaded a comfortable day bed. The guys had slaved over the outdoor space to transform it into an oasis in the middle of the city.

It hadn't been quite hot enough before now for them to enjoy it, but she was looking forward to the rest of spring and cookouts and the refreshment the cool water would bring during the steamiest days of their future.

If she could fix what she had broken by reassuring the man she'd inadvertently injured with her insecurity and fears. Holly neared Lorenzo, approaching slowly. He didn't turn to face her.

"I'm sorry, Lorenzo."

"Oh, you're still here? Need me to call a cab?" he asked, deadpan. As if he didn't give a shit one way or the other.

Okay, fine. She'd let him have that one jab.

"You can't get rid of me that easily." She took a deep breath, then admitted, "I got scared. Just for a minute. What you need to understand is that I would have been back, even if Trent and Owen hadn't been there to stop me from messing things up entirely. I'll always come back to you."

She stepped closer and reached way up to lay her hand on the knotted muscles at his shoulder. Damn, he was tense.

He shrugged her off. Her stomach did flip-flops. What if she'd broken his trust one time too many?

"What are you going to do if Trent goes away?" His question was strangled, as if he could barely force it out. "Losing him for years will be bad enough. If you go with him, if we're not enough to keep you on our own—"

"Don't even say that." Holly couldn't bear the thought of Trent surrounded by concrete and steel instead of their loving arms.

"I don't want to. I don't even want to think it. But it could happen!" He whirled then, slicing his hands through the air between them. "And then what?"

"Then we ride it out together." She opened her arms, and though he didn't step into them, neither did he evade her when she advanced, putting them around him and hugging him tight. "I might need a moment to breathe every once in a while, but nothing can take me away from you. Or Owen. With or without Trent, I want you."

Air whooshed out of him, ruffling her hair. "You do?"

"Yeah, turns out I'm a hot guy hoarder. What can I say?" She smiled wryly as she peeked up at him. "Of course, that means I want him and Owen too. But that doesn't dictate what I feel for you. Lorenzo, I love you. You know that, right?"

His head canted to one side, making his gorgeous onyx hair shift in the sunlight until it seemed almost blue.

He stared down into her wide-open eyes for the space of a ragged breath, and then two. "What did you say?"

"You heard me." Why wasn't he saying it back?

"Say it again." He held onto her, his fingers flexing where moments before they'd been limp and defeated.

This time she didn't second guess, and she certainly didn't backtrack or run. She shouted up to the sky, "I love Lorenzo! You hear me, universe? I love him. And Owen. And Trent. So fuck you if you think you're going to break us apart. It's not happening. *I love them!*"

When she opened her eyes, panting, emotion pouring out of her as if she'd ripped the scab off a not-quite-healed sore, Lorenzo was grinning.

"What?" she asked. Her face burned and not from the desert sun.

"You're adorable as fuck when you get riled up." He took her into her arms and lifted her so that her toes dangled several inches off the ground.

"Hey. What are you doing?" She squirmed, but he squashed her attempts to escape. Instead, he strode through the crushed red rocks and pinned her against the back fence. It surprised her, yeah. But scared her? Never. Not in his arms.

"I'm going to show you that you're mine. Ours." He leaned into her. "You're not going anywhere, are you? Not today, and not ever."

His body screened her, shielded her, from anyone who might have been peeking into the yard. That was good, so they couldn't see the way her body responded instantly to his dominance. Her nipples drew tight and she would swear she got wet in record time. "I said I wasn't."

"Good. Because Holly, whether it's smart or not..."

Lorenzo bit her neck, inspiring her to raise her legs and wrap them around his waist. "I love you too. Damn you."

"I'll take that." She arched against him, wishing it were possible to get even closer than they already were. The explosive tension of the confrontation in the kitchen, the fear, the anxiety, all of it required an outlet, and she was pretty sure he'd be willing to provide it for her.

"Yes, you will." He reached down and encircled her wrists with his fingers before pinning her arms beside her head. "See, even if you had run, I would have chased you. My ex might have left me, but I let her go because I knew deep down, it wasn't meant to be. With you... No, I'd fight for you."

"You would?" She should probably be appalled by his barbarism. But she'd be lying if she said it didn't make her want him more. To be claimed by him in such a way that it erased her fear that they could be torn apart.

What happened between them—her and Lorenzo, as well as the whole group together—would shape their futures. And she knew now that those paths would be the same.

"Yeah." He wasn't gentle when he took her mouth.

Then he showed her exactly what he meant by claiming she belonged to him. Her body responded to his every touch, bending and flaring with each connection they made. Suddenly, there weren't nearly enough of those to suit her.

"Maybe we should go inside," she suggested between kisses.

"Too far." He growled against her skin. "I've waited long enough to have you to myself."

"Is that what you want?" She wished her hands were free so she could run her fingers through his thick mane.

"Sometimes. I love sharing you, being part of something bigger, but it's about more than that."

"For me too," she whispered.

"This is one of those times." He let go of her long enough to wedge one hand between them and straight down the front of her pants. He found her pussy and the places she needed his touch most, as though he had made love to her thousands of times instead of only a few.

"What if the neighbors see? What if one of the security guys does?"

"So what?" Lorenzo clearly didn't give a shit. "They can get a good look at my ass any time they pony up the cover charge at the club. So they should consider it a freebie. A community service."

"The police might not agree, and they're all over Trent already."

"It'd be worth a misdemeanor charge to be inside you right now." He grazed his stubbled jaw over her cheek, the prickles only making her need him more.

So Holly didn't object when he shoved her pants down to mid-thigh and flashed her a wicked grin when he discovered she wasn't wearing underwear beneath them.

"Besides." He allowed a hint of his usual laidback facade through his very serious demeanor then. "Your mom forgave Trent for getting you kidnapped, so she'll probably be nice enough to bail us out."

Horrified, Holly couldn't even think about that. Her face, crumpled in horror, must have been apparent.

Lorenzo cracked up. Thank God he wasn't still mad, or worse—hurt. "In any case, I'm pretty sure the secret agent dudes and lady out front are more likely to cheer us on than call the cops to report us."

She got the feeling he was probably right about that.

Lorenzo twisted his hand and unsnapped his jeans with a flick of his fingers.

"Do they have stripper school for that or what?" she teased.

Thankfully, his quick smile and even faster attraction was back, wiping away the last of his melancholy. "I know all kinds of tricks."

Holly was almost—but not quite—afraid to ask. "Like what?"

"I can easily make you come without taking any more of your clothes off, remember?"

Eventually, maybe. *Easily*? Nah. Holly couldn't help it, she rolled her eyes at him. And that was all it took.

Lorenzo grabbed her ass, and hoisted her up farther against the fence so that her pelvis was aligned with his. Then he reclaimed her arms and nailed them to the fence. He kissed her as he danced, to music only he could hear, rubbing the bulge of his hard cock over her pussy. Despite the fact that he hadn't entered her yet, she knew he was going to win this war of wills.

His body felt so good against hers, solid and so damn hot he heated her from the inside out.

His hair fell forward, framing their faces and making her forget that anything existed outside the two of them and the intimate moment they were sharing. Lorenzo kissed her, his mouth stealing over hers, his tongue sparring with hers before he moved away again.

And when he came up for air, he bit her lower lip just enough to make her pussy clench, wishing she had him to hold on to. His hips kept rocking, making sure he rode the furrow between her legs. His erection nudged her clit at the peak of each stroke.

Did he do this to women at the club? Was that why he made so damn much money?

And would she care if he kept doing it now?

Holly blinked, trying not to let reality steal her enjoyment. Too late. Her breathing slowed and her legs loosened around him.

"That's not how this works," he told her. Lorenzo pressed harder, grinding on her and making her wetter despite her attempts to flee before he overwhelmed her. This time there was nowhere to run. Between Lorenzo and the fence at her back, she was trapped. Forced to confront the situation.

"How does it work exactly?" she asked, her voice breathy. "Do women tip you extra for lap dances if they come on you?"

He froze. "They used to. But I haven't gone off the stage in about a month."

"Oh." Holly closed her eyes. "I'm sorry I'm such a bitch today."

Instead of dropping her or berating her, Lorenzo smiled. "Jealous?"

"Maybe," she admitted.

"You don't want anyone else to have this cock? Only you?" He rubbed up against her again, this time with faster jabs of his hips that made her eyes fly open once more.

"Yeah." Holly didn't care if it was selfish, given that he shared her with his best friends so seamlessly. It was the truth.

"Good. Because you're the only one I want to give it to, and I'm going to make you love every minute of it when I finally do." He kissed down her neck, his hips adding a circle at the top of every stroke. Her thighs quivered around him, and she knew they weren't going to be exposed long out there in the backyard.

Because she was about to surrender by coming before he'd even tried to press into her.

"Go ahead." It was more of an order than an invitation. "Prove me right and I'll reward us both. I'm going to fuck you so good, Holly."

No fair. She couldn't resist the combination of his confidence, his prowess, and his desire. A ball of pleasure slammed into her core then rippled outward, making every bit of her it expanded through shudder and clench. Even her teeth clicked together as she writhed in his hold.

Lorenzo didn't stop and he definitely didn't drop her.

As soon as she came, she felt him shift. His hand left her arm long enough to spear between them again, freeing his cock from his underwear. Before she'd stopped spasming, he began to penetrate the pulsing rings of muscle at her entrance.

It felt so good that Holly repeated his name in a guttural chant as he drove up into her.

The fence behind her creaked.

She hoped it held, but not even the mental image of them crashing, still fucking, into the neighbor's yard and getting a million splinters in sensitive places was going to keep her from welcoming him inside her then.

"Fuck yes," he growled. "You belong here, don't you, Holly? With me. With us. In our beds and our lives. Don't ever fool yourself into thinking otherwise."

When he punctuated his demands with a nip on her neck, she shuddered, another mini orgasm washing over her as he pumped into her.

He wasn't rough, but he was all-consuming. His strokes were glides, not painful thrusts. Unrelenting, they drove her wild as she was impaled on his thick cock. She milked him, coming again—or still—as he rode her, unleashing his doubts and the pain of nearly breaking apart as he fused them together as tightly as he could.

"Damn, Holly. You feel so good. So right. We fit. Don't you see that?" He nearly begged as he filled her so full she could hardly do anything but cry out his name over and over. Her nails dug into his shoulders as she tried to spur him on.

"I do." She gasped when he hit a particularly sensitive spot inside her.

"Right there?" he grunted

"Yeah." Holly panted each time he did it. "Yeah. Yeah."

Then she was exploding, thankful for the wooden slats behind her, keeping her upright when the entire world went out of focus. She would have screamed if he weren't there to swallow the blatantly sexual sound she made as she wrung his dick dry.

Lorenzo shuddered as he joined her, freezing, locked deep before unloading within her. His balls tapped her pussy as he jerked, emptying himself. The entire time, he stared into her eyes, letting her see that no matter what happened, he was never going to run out on her.

And neither was she.

Never again.

Lorenzo braced himself with one straight-locked arm against the fence, his chest heaving as he basked in the remnants of his orgasm the same way she had the sunlight when she'd emerged from the house. After a minute or maybe two, he slipped from her body.

Wobbly, Holly fixed her shorts, then sank to her knees. Lorenzo's hands dropped to his cock, slick with their mingled pleasure and tried to tuck it into his pants, but she must have really gotten to him because suave, practiced Lorenzo couldn't seem to manage the simple task by himself.

Holly leaned in and kissed the head of his cock, then did it for him. She sat on her haunches as she rested her head on his thigh and peered up at him, grinning.

She couldn't wait to tell Trent and Owen that they'd fucked and made up. Maybe the other two would want to celebrate with them next. Just as soon as they caught their breath.

When Lorenzo had, he put his hands beneath her arms and lifted her to her feet.

"Did you like knowing someone could have seen us?" Holly arched a brow.

"Uh huh."

"Maybe I'll have Trent and Owen bring me to the club next time you're working so you can roam free of the stage again." She winked. "I hear I have some cash in my bank account these days. I can afford a big tip if you give me a proper lap dance in front of everyone so they can see what we already know: I do belong to you. To all three of you, and you're mine too."

He groaned.

Somehow the thought of being that woman, the kind who could ask a man at a club for his services and enjoy them right there, anyone watching be damned... well, that sounded like the stuff of one of her wildest fantasies. They made her into the person she'd only wished, before she'd met them, she could someday become.

"Hey, lovebirds!" one of their security guards, Holly thought it was the guy they called Ransom, shouted at them. Both of them jumped before glancing, guilty as fuck, in that direction.

"Is that what you call them? I was thinking more along the lines of horny toads," Sevan joked as she peeked from between her own two lovers.

"When you're in love, you gotta do what you gotta do." Levi shrugged. Holly should ask them how they seemed to understand her struggle so well sometime. What was their story? "But now that you've gotten that out of your systems, can you please get those fine asses back inside?"

Lorenzo laughed as Holly hid her face against his shoulder. He saluted their babysitters, then swung her into his arms and carried her into the house in time to see Trent and Owen turn toward them. But when she expected them to take advantage of her lingering arousal and the state Lorenzo had put her in, instead she realized they'd been a different sort of fired up.

They were angry, and had been arguing.

Because of her?

Oh shit.

Holly twisted until Lorenzo set her down so she could try to make things right between them all. *Please, let this work.* It would be just her luck to find the three loves of her life, just in time for them to break apart.

17

———

Trent couldn't remember the last time he'd argued with Owen. They never really fought unless it was about dumb shit like what movie to watch or where to order dinner from, and never with any real heat. But the moment he'd hung up the phone with the executive liaison at the bank, Owen had lit into him.

"I can't believe you did that!" Owen roared.

"Why does it matter? You were my friend before I had that money. Aren't you going to be now that I'm broke again?" Trent tried not to let his disappointment show, but his whole life he'd had to wonder if people liked him for him or for what he could do for them. He'd thought things were different with his friends, but that didn't mean they would be okay with sacrificing like he had.

"I should fucking punch you for saying stupid shit like that." Owen's hands fisted at his side. "First, you deserved that money. It was rightfully yours. You love Holly. Your marriage isn't fake. And you met all the terms of the trust. But mostly, it makes you look guilty as hell!"

Oh. Well, he hadn't thought of that.

Trent's ire flared, his face burning, as the back door opened and Lorenzo carried Holly into their home. From the residual wobbliness of her legs when he set her down, their entwined fingers, and their flushed faces—not to mention the eyeful he'd gotten when he glanced out the window while on the phone—it was clear they at least had made up.

Good, because he was going to need their cool heads and interpersonal skills to smooth over the bumps he'd made with Owen.

Holly stopped short when she picked up on the tension in the room, but Lorenzo was still blinking as his eyes adjusted to the interior after the blazing sun and Holly's brightness outside.

"Okay, now that that's settled. What are we going to do about your mom? You can't just let her have her way after she played so dirty with Holly. There's no way in hell we're letting her win." Lorenzo clutched Holly to his side as they neared. Trent didn't blame the guy. And seeing the way both of his best friends had bonded with her in his absence made him sure he had done the right thing for them all, even if they didn't agree right at first.

"Too late. I gave the money back."

"You did what?" Lorenzo gaped.

"Gave. It. Back." Trent grimaced. "It was nothing but trouble. I knew I never should have taken it in the first place. And now it's gone. My mother can keep her damn empire. That's all she has left."

"But the patents and your company..." Holly put her hand in front of her mouth and her eyes shimmered. And finally he understood. It wasn't because he was significantly poorer than he'd been, twice now in his life, but because she was afraid he'd lost his shot at pursuing his dream.

For the first time in his life, he was surrounded by people who loved him and wanted nothing more than for him to succeed. In his book, he was the richest man on earth.

"I already told him he's an idiot." Owen threw up his hands, then let them slap against the sides of his legs as they fell. "There's a twenty-four hour wait time on the transaction. Can someone please talk some sense into him before I do it with my foot up his ass?"

"The business will be fine." Trent held out his hand and she came to him. So he tugged her to his side, looped an arm around her, and kissed her cheek. "We're going to be, too. This isn't going to change as much as you think."

"How do you figure?" Owen glared.

"If this was only about the money, I'd have taken my inheritance and invested it in something safe. This is about doing work that means something to me. About giving back all the time. About taking what I have and making it enough, more than enough. That's what I really want. It was never about the money. It's about spending my life for the greater good. I know it sounds ridiculous, but I want to change the world."

"You've already changed mine." Holly smiled up at him.

"Thank you." Trent put his face in his hand. "I'm probably being selfish by doing it this way because I also like the thought of building things from the ground up like I was before my dad died. Besides, I can't see any other solution."

"Whatever it takes, we're with you," Holly promised, then looked over at Owen and Lorenzo, who were nodding. "Somehow we'll get through this and back on track. We'll think of something. Some way to get through this as long as you're not in trouble. Your mom will drop the charges now, right?"

Even she didn't sound entirely convinced. In the ominous stillness, the ringing of Trent's phone jarred them all. Trent answered before it could rattle his nerves again. "Hello?"

"What are you doing over there? Your account manager at the bank just called to verify the directive you called in." Ford asked, sounding only slightly annoyed. "Don't you think you should consult with your lawyers before making such drastic moves?"

"Not when they're the right thing for everyone I love," Trent responded without hesitation.

"And what about you?" Kari asked from the other end of the line. "Holly isn't going to be able to be happy if you're not okay, too. Even if you let that transfer go through, you're short some cash. Your mom is a selfish piece of shit. She'll come after you for the rest of the money. You know she will."

Ford chimed in. "I don't think Kari's wrong, but I do think she'll only be wasting some of her precious funds if she does. There's no way you're going down for that when you're legally entitled to the money and I've heard from an inside source that they have more than enough to nail her on the kidnapping conspiracy. Here's what I think you should do."

Everyone stood still barely breathing.

"Instead of sending it back to your mother, donate it. Let's say half of it goes to research on kidney disease and support of families fighting the disease, including the funds already allocated to Holly's mom. The rest could be earmarked for funding green energy solutions."

Owen grinned. "I'd had a similar thought, but not one that genius. This way Trent could still tap into some of it for startup costs and Holly's mom is in the clear. Meanwhile if his mother tries to come after him, she'll look bad to the rest of the socialites, which would never do."

Holly melted against Trent so he propped her up.

He looked down at the woman in his arms, who nodded and hugged him tighter. "I'm good if you are. We'll figure the rest out so we can keep going on our research before someone else beats us to it. Especially now that the schematics will be on record with the patent applications, it will be important to move quickly."

"What if you got an infusion of cash from angel investors to bridge the gap or, hell, to increase your funding beyond even what your inheritance was?" Brady asked.

"Venture capital?" Trent groaned. "I didn't want a bunch of opinions watering down my ideas. But I guess, if we have to..."

"The man said angel investors." Josh jumped in. "And if you take our money, we'll let you do whatever you want with it. You were doing just fine on your own. Well, actually, I take that back...with Holly's help. So my one stipulation is that you hire her on as the head engineer of your company."

"What?" Trent could hardly breathe.

"Are you saying *you* want to invest in Trent's inventions?" Holly asked.

"Of course they do, girl!" Kari cheered. "They'd be

dumb not to get in on that, and my guys are anything but stupid."

Lorenzo and Owen both came closer, waving their hands and nodding their heads.

Trent couldn't speak past the knot in his throat.

So Holly did it for him. "Thank you, all of you, so much."

She buried her face against Trent's chest, which gave him the strength to accept his friends' generous offer. "You're sure?"

Owen and Lorenzo shot him looks like he was nuts. He probably was, but how could everything be coming together so perfectly? To be able to do this on his own, without his family's money making it possible, was everything he'd been working toward before the world had turned upside down a month ago.

"Absolutely." Ford didn't seem to have a shred of doubt. "You're going to make us even richer, and help a lot of people while you're doing it."

Trent could only think of one reason he would say no.

"So what do you say, Holly? Will you do it? Will you accept the position as head engineer and as our wife? For real. Nothing fake about it?" Trent stared down into her eyes, which turned a bit glassy with unshed tears.

"On one condition." Holly propped her hand on her waist, making Trent sure he'd agree to anything to have her on his team.

"Which is?"

"The first five million I make in salary and from the stock options you're giving me as part of my sign-on package, I'm paying back into the fund you're going to set up for kidney disease patients and research efforts."

"I didn't lend that money to you, I gave it to you." He

would have argued, but Lorenzo and Owen were shooting him glares that said they'd never forgive him if he fucked this up.

"Those are my terms." Holly backed up a step. Though it was away from him, it was closer to Owen and Lorenzo. She reached out and took one of their hands in each of hers. "We do this together, on even footing, or not at all."

"You know, she's right." Trent nodded.

"Um, guys. She's always going to be right." Kari sounded as if she was rolling her eyes. "You might as well get used to that now."

They all laughed, but Holly the most.

"We're going to need reps and technicians and stuff too if you guys want in on this." Trent turned to Lorenzo and Owen. He didn't want them to think that Holly got preferential treatment. He cared for all three of them, and if they could do this together...they might just have a shot at the life they'd all hoped for but couldn't quite believe could be possible.

"I'm in. Besides, Lorenzo's getting too old for stripping anyway." Owen smirked.

"Hey!" Lorenzo swiped at him, but Owen dodged.

"See? You're slow, old man." Owen laughed until Lorenzo got him back.

"Let's see who can last longer in bed, huh? Then we'll talk about who's the old man."

Holly's brows rose.

Ford cleared his throat. "It sounds like you might have some celebrating to do. So say yes, and let us get off the phone so we can start doing what we need to keep Trent's ass out of jail, his mother annoyed, and lots of people on their way to a better life. Do we have a deal?"

Trent looked at Holly, Lorenzo, and Owen, taking his

time and thinking through each of their situations before he drew a deep breath and said, "We do. And thank you."

"No need," Brady said as a clap came in the background. Were they high-fiving over their part of the bargain? "We're going to be the ones thanking you before this is over. I'm sure of it."

"We love you," Kari called as they wrapped things up. "Call Andi and me later, Holly. Way later. Go...be together."

It was wild to have someone understand exactly what was important in his life and to his soul. So Trent took his friends' advice and hung up so he could show his wife and her lovers exactly how he was feeling about them in that moment.

18

For a minute, they stood there, staring at the phone as if trying to wrap their heads around everything that had just happened.

"I don't have all the answers. I don't know what the future is going to bring. But if we're in this together, we have a better chance of making it through and getting where we want to be. I do know that." Trent put one hand on Lorenzo's shoulder and the other on Owen's. The guys huddled around, with Holly at their center.

"I'm already there." She looked up at them with a smile that wasn't even forced. Despite the news and the drastic changes in her world, she felt rock solid when near her three incredible men.

"Well, just in case you get locked up, maybe we should fool around one more time so you have some fond memories to see you through the lonely nights," Lorenzo teased.

"Hey, quit that." She pinched his nipple. "Ford, Brady, and Josh aren't going to let that happen."

The guys definitely had a different sense of humor

than she did. Instead of being horrified, Trent seemed relieved. Maybe Lorenzo's jokes took away some of the seriousness of the situation.

Either way, Trent said, "Yeah. That's a good idea. I don't plan to have sex with anyone not in the room for the rest of my life. Besides, I'm not really into anal, unless I'm the one doing the fucking."

Holly shivered because they both knew how good it could be.

But so did Owen. He shocked her by winking then saying, "Hey, don't knock butt stuff until you try it."

Lorenzo whipped his stare to Owen and then to Holly, who high-fived Owen. They could learn, they could grow together, and they could teach each other how to live their best lives. She laughed and tried to hug her three guys at once, but they were a lot for one woman's arms.

Trent watched them with something more than friendship or relief in his eyes. There was heat and longing that only one thing was going to fulfill. She didn't even see him move, but suddenly the world flipped upside down as he put her over his shoulder and the four of them migrated to his room without a word of instruction necessary.

By the time she'd hit the bed and bounced a few times, Owen and Lorenzo were mostly naked. They worked together to rid her of her pajamas while Trent stripped, giving her plenty of eye candy with his long, lean body.

"Why do I get the feeling you two weren't really kidding around out there?" Trent looked between Holly and Owen.

"Because we had one hell of a morning yesterday. Didn't we, Owen?" Holly shoved him onto his back and crawled between his legs, unable to stop from smirking as she took in his eager gaze and his rock-hard cock, which definitely wasn't going to make it believable even if he tried to call her a liar.

"Yeah. We did." He put his hands under her shoulders and pulled her up so her face was level with his dick. He didn't have to ask. She licked along his shaft, making him shudder.

"Do you want this?" Trent pulled a package from his nightstand. Inside was a purple plug with a flared base. "I bought it for Holly, but maybe..."

"It *is* for me. Anything that makes you guys enjoy our time together more means I love it too." She took the package from him and showed it to Owen. "Wouldn't it feel amazing to wear this while I go down on you?"

He groaned. "Yeah. But... You guys don't think it's weird? And you get that I'm not into you two, right?"

Trent laughed and doubled over, making Owen's cock lose some of its stiffness.

When Lorenzo smacked Trent's gut with the back of his hand, he stopped. "Sorry. Sorry. I'm only laughing because of course I know you're not into us and it wouldn't freak me out even if you were. Wait. Were you seriously worried? Have you been hiding this because you think we wouldn't understand?"

Lorenzo muttered, "Idiot."

"Do whatever you like best." Trent shrugged. "And if you ever again imply that I'd be some kind of judgmental prick about it, I'll be offended. I'll give you this one for free because I see you were really in your head about it. Damn, Owen."

Owen scrubbed his hand over his face, then ripped at the package. Holly figured it said something about his desire that he was able to get it open with his bare hands, and in a hurry too.

While he caught the lube Trent tossed him and slicked the silicone, she took him into her mouth again and started to get him fully hard. Except it wasn't until she accepted the toy from him and began to slide it into his welcoming body as she sucked his cock that he grew in her mouth to his full length and girth.

"Damn, maybe I should have bought one for myself." Trent came up behind Holly, her ass in the air as she serviced Owen. "Since you both seem to like it so much."

Lorenzo made a sound of agreement. Owen relaxed as his friends cheered them on, as she'd known they would.

From behind her, Trent kept talking, only turning her on more. "Holly likes it too, Owen. She's soaked."

He dipped a finger inside her, then withdrew it slowly before showing it to their friend. Owen thrust upward into her mouth, making her choke a little even as she slid the plug to its base in his ass. She gave it a test tug. It wasn't going anywhere.

"Are you going to fuck her or what?" Owen asked. "Between the stuff that happened this morning and having everything I've ever wanted, this is feeling a bit too good."

"There's no such thing," Lorenzo reassured their friend. "But I'll even the score for you."

Holly couldn't see exactly how he contorted himself into position, but somehow he ended up on his back between hers and Trent's legs so he could fit his talented mouth to her pussy. He concentrated on her clit, making her moan around Owen's shaft.

Owen speared his fingers into her hair and held her steady so he could fuck up into her mouth, doing all the work while she concentrated on accepting the pleasure Lorenzo rained on her clit with his lips and tongue.

If she could have, she would have asked Trent to fuck her. But she didn't need to—he was there, fitting the blunt tip of his cock to her pussy. He cursed as he pressed into her heat and slickness, working her open so she could take him deeper on every forward pass. She wondered if he could tell that Lorenzo had been there not so long ago and if that fired him up as much as it did her.

He started out slowly, plunging balls-deep into her each time she swallowed Owen, only to withdraw entirely before doing it again. It didn't take very long before that wasn't enough for either of them, and he began to pump steadily inside her, filling her with his thick cock.

It felt incredible, but it wasn't enough. She reached with one hand for her breast, but Trent swiped it away, replacing it with his own.

"Make her come, Lorenzo. Distract her so I can get in her ass." Trent slapped her flank then, only spurring her on. "Once she has me, you can take over for me in this pussy. She's so tight. You're going to love being back in there."

He growled against her flesh and redoubled his efforts, guaranteeing she would yield to them. Holly didn't even try to fight the rapture they gifted her with. Instead she embraced it and flew, crashing into an orgasm so powerful she wasn't sure how Trent thought he was going leverage it to open her to him.

She squeezed him from her body with the powerful waves of her orgasm. But he was back in seconds, using the relief that followed to gain admittance to her body.

He was slippery and hard as steel as he sank into her ass.

Lorenzo's gentle sucking on her pussy felt so good that if there was even a twinge of discomfort, she didn't dwell on it. Owen lifted her off his cock while Trent advanced, fitting himself inside her. Holly cried out, but only because she wanted more. She needed to have all three of them inside her at once, occupying her completely.

Trent wrapped his arms around her, fondling her breasts for a few moments before he rolled, taking her with him. He landed on his back, with her lying on top of him, his chest glued to her back. Lorenzo didn't hesitate. He pounced on her and tucked himself against her slick pussy, working into her before she'd even finished enduring the aftershocks of the first orgasm they'd given her.

They stretched her, spread her, and made her feel things straight to her soul.

And that was even before Owen knelt beside Trent's shoulder and tipped her head in his direction. Trent held her hips as he screwed into her from below and presented her to Lorenzo so he could do the same. They fucked her relentlessly, driving her up again before she'd had a chance to settle.

Holly opened her mouth and wordlessly invited Owen inside. He gave her something to do with her excess energy as she licked, sucked, and bobbed on his erection. With one hand, she reached between his legs, first to fondle his tight sac and then to press on the base of the plug that did to him what Trent was doing to her. It had to feel as good too, because his thighs quivered before her eyes.

Trent was kissing her shoulder, traveling toward her neck as he set the pace for them all. Though not frantic, it was urgent, and demanding. And when he raked his teeth over the column of her neck, she clamped down around all three men who possessed her body and her heart.

"Ah fuck." Owen held her head still as he began to piston between her lips. "I'm close already."

"Me too," Lorenzo groaned. "You're so gorgeous like this, Holly. So giving and so voracious. I love it. I love you."

Trent murmured in her ear, "You were made for us. Show him, Holly. Show him how much you love it when we fuck you like this. When we become one, like we were always meant to be."

Owen reached forward and cupped her breast, flicking his thumb over her nipple.

That was it. She lost control of her own body, of her mind too. All she could do was take what they were giving her, relish every moment, and every scrap of bliss. She didn't have to hoard it, though, or hope it went on forever, because she knew that with them, every night of their lives was going to be filled with this much love, passion, and friendship.

Holly came so hard her vision went white. She screamed something barely intelligible about how she loved them, and maybe their names, around Owen's jerking cock as they shouted hers and flooded her with their own epic releases.

Her body absorbed it all, making them part of her as she was already part of them.

They were in this together. Four love. For life.

19

———

"I shouldn't be surprised that they have a gorgeous catamaran like this one," Lorenzo purred, obviously in love with Ford, Brady, Josh, and Kari's yacht at first sight.

"Have you ever been on a boat like this before?" Owen asked Lorenzo.

Holly figured Trent had, though he still seemed suitably impressed. Maybe when they sold their first million units, they could get themselves something like this...well, not as grand, but a boat of some sort so they could spend lazy days out to sea, entertaining themselves far away from the rest of the world.

"Nah, but I used to sit on the docks at home and watch them. I'd wonder where they came from and where they were going next. I never thought I'd find myself traveling as far from home as some of them." Lorenzo held Holly's hand as he followed the mast of the catamaran all the way up to where it seemed to pierce the sky.

"Maybe you're home now," Holly said softly as she

looked first to him, then Owen, and finally Trent, who was smiling at her. It wasn't a new thing. She caught him staring often during the days they spent working on their company together.

"Wherever you three are is where I'm meant to be." Lorenzo kissed her knuckles.

Holly fixed her dress and strolled with them to the trampolines, where her mother was already sitting on one of the foam cube seats that had been arranged for their closest friends and family. To see her there, her hair blowing in the breeze, and a smile on her face as she talked to her neighbors without being out of breath, made everything perfect.

Trent squeezed her fingers on the opposite side of her from Lorenzo. She glanced over at him and flashed him a smile. He'd made this possible, even if he'd deny it.

Together they took the four seats behind her mother and lost themselves in friendly conversation interspersed with heated glances and casual touches that promised the romantic mood would lead to an incredible night together later.

"Not to interrupt, but would you four mind being less sickeningly perfect?" a man on the opposite side of them said with a rueful grin. He stuck out his hand and said, "I'm Max Green. Kari's old neighbor, from the days when she was slumming it with regular folk like me."

Trent chuckled and shook his hand before the rest of them did too.

"I remember Kari telling me about you." Holly tried not to wince as she recalled the trouble they'd been through. "You rescued her from her stalker."

"Nah." Max shrugged. "I mostly stood around with her until the police came. She did all the brave stuff herself."

"Where's your date?" Holly's mom asked.

"Mom!" Holly elbowed her lightly.

Max only laughed. "Like I said, some of you have all the luck. I'm starting to think I've been looking for the wrong things, though."

"You're living on the edge, saying that to Holly and her mom." Lorenzo pointed at them. "They're going to be setting you up every Friday for the rest of your life if you're not careful."

"If it's with women as lovely as them, I'd be thrilled." Max obviously didn't need as much help as he was pretending. He already had her mother on his side. "So are you four going next? You can probably bribe Andi to officiate for you at half price."

They all laughed. Owen said, "Nah. Holly and Trent are already married."

"But I didn't get to see my baby in a white dress or help her plan a party to celebrate how amazing the four of you are together." Holly's mom pouted.

"We haven't really had time to think about that," Trent said, the corners of his mouth tugging downward. "I'm sorry I didn't, though. Would you guys be into it?"

Holly held her breath. She'd wanted to ask that question herself but was afraid it could trigger bad memories for Lorenzo.

Owen and Lorenzo smirked at each other before Lorenzo said, "Hell, yes."

So she leaned over and kissed him, then Owen, drawing a few envious stares from the other guests while Andi beamed at them from her place of honor at the bow of the boat. Damn straight, her men were fine. "I love you guys, and I would be proud to shout it out to all our friends and family some time."

She'd be lying if she didn't agree a bit with her mom. Though she'd ended up with all the really important things, a real wedding where they celebrated their joint commitment with their friends and family would be...special.

"Maybe next time we do a test on our equipment on one of those really sunny islands, we should have a beach wedding," Owen suggested.

Lorenzo nodded. "I'd like that too. Something different from my last one. Less formal and more natural, more honest. Perfect and beautiful, just like you."

Holly's mom beamed at Lorenzo. "That's right, honey. You tell my daughter how amazing she is."

"Hey, I thought I was your favorite," Trent joked. He often told Holly's mother she was his chosen mom. Their bond warmed Holly's heart, since the chances of him reconciling with his own mother were pretty much zip. She hadn't taken very well to life in prison, where she was awaiting trial for kidnapping and blackmail charges. But today wasn't the day to think about that.

"You're my favorite son-in-law." Mom grinned. "They're tied for favorite son-in-law-to-be."

Holly laughed, thrilled to have all of her most favorite people together in one place, happy, healthy, and ready to cheer on her friends, who had found the same for themselves.

As they waited for Kari to emerge, Lorenzo and Trent began to chat with the partners on the other side of them, who recognized Trent and Holly from the news segments they'd been featured on lately. Their company was blossoming, the solar and battery technology performing even better than they'd hoped, and all the paperwork was in place to begin full-scale production following the beta tests they were currently conducting.

"Not to mix business and pleasure, but could I give you my card?" The man handed over a thick off-white rectangle with gold embossing. "I've been impressed with what I've seen so far, and if you could give me a bit more information and an in-person demo, I think my company would be excited to put in an order. Will you be offering discounts for bulk buys?"

Owen had been heading up the sales division while Lorenzo focused on technical installations. So Owen responded. "It depends. How many units would you be looking for? Given our pledge to community donations that match our commercial sales, we wouldn't likely be able to drop our price unless you could commit to a thousand or more at a time."

"I was thinking more like a million." The man smirked. "I own hotels all over the world, and our best estimates are that we could save enough to pay back the panels and batteries within seven years at our tropical locations. Plus, the positive press from your charity policies won't hurt either. Maybe we could arrange for the donated equipment to go to locals in the communities around our resorts."

Lorenzo slapped Owen on the back when his jaw hung open. He glanced at the name on the card in his hand and his eyes widened a bit. "Oh. Yes, sir. Let's set up a time to discuss this..."

"Later. Sounds good." The man smiled and shook each of their hands. "But first, I think the beautiful bride is nearly ready."

Holly sat up straighter as Andi took a sip of water then straightened her dress, her guys sitting in the front row, watching as Ford, Cooper, and Brady formed a line off to her left. Holly knew Kari was getting ready to come into view by the way the guys squared their shoulders. All three were laser focused on the area to the side of the cockpit.

When Kari appeared, wearing a gossamer white dress with a mile-long embroidered veil that fluttered picturesquely in the light but constant wind, Holly thought she'd never seen something as romantic or beautiful as her friend about to promise the rest of her life in exchange for the same from her three lovers.

Holly didn't even bother to hide the tears of joy that rolled down her face during the ceremony. The entire crowd got to their feet, clapping and hooting as the happy quartet sealed their promises to each other with a round of passionate kisses. Beside them, Max sniffled, making her wish everyone could be as fortunate as her, Kari, Andi, and their men.

Then her guys were there, Lorenzo brushing away the damp trails on her cheeks as Owen and Trent circled around her.

"I never believed there could be someone like that for me. I've never been so glad to be wrong in my life," Trent said to her before he kissed her tenderly. Lorenzo and Owen piled on, wrapping their arms around them until she was the center of an epic group hug.

"I love you. All three of you." Holly spun around, finding heaven in every direction.

"I love you," they replied at the same time.

A loud pop startled them all, and she looked over just in time to see her mother, who had stepped over to the bar nearby, raising an overflowing bottle of champagne in their direction. "Who's ready to drink to that?"

"I'll take two," Max said as he shoved a glass under the fountain of foam. "Or three."

Holly and her guys laughed, danced, and lived together until the dark clouds of their past were burned away by the power of the sun and their undying love for each other.

Want to know more about Andi, Cooper, Reed, and Simon or Kari's billionaire boyfriends? You're in luck! One-click now to read their stories, too.

THE 4-EVER DUET (Andi)
4-Ever Mine
4-Ever Theirs

THE EVER AFTER DUET (Kari)
Fourplay
Fourkeeps

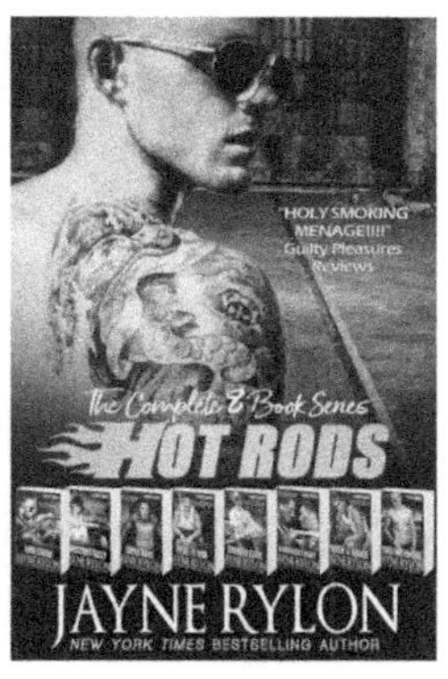

If you enjoy Jayne's menage stories, but missed out on the Powertools: Hot Rods series, you can buy all eight books in a discounted single-volume boxset by clicking HERE.

CLAIM A $5 GIFT CERTIFICATE

Jayne is so sure you will love her books, she'd like you to try any one of your choosing for free. Claim your $5 gift certificate by signing up for her newsletter. You'll also learn about freebies, new releases, extras, appearances, and more!

www.jaynerylon.com/newsletter

WHAT WAS YOUR FAVORITE PART?

Did you enjoy this book? If so, please leave a review and tell your friends about it. Word of mouth and online reviews are immensely helpful and greatly appreciated.

JAYNE'S SHOP

Check out Jayne's online shop for autographed print books, direct download ebooks, reading-themed apparel up to size 5XL, mugs, tote bags, notebooks, Mr. Rylon's wood (you'll have to see it for yourself!) and more.
www.jaynerylon.com/shop

LISTEN UP!

The majority of Jayne's books are also available in audio format on Audible, Amazon, iTunes, Hoopla, Chirp, and other audiobook retailers.

ABOUT THE AUTHOR

Jayne Rylon is a *New York Times* and *USA Today* bestselling author who has sold more than one million books. She has received numerous industry awards including the Romantic Times Reviewers' Choice Award for Best Indie Erotic Romance and the Swirl Award, which recognizes excellence in diverse romance. She is an Honor Roll member of the Romance Writers of America. Her stories used to begin as daydreams in seemingly endless business meetings, but now she is a full time author, who employs the skills she learned from her straight-laced corporate existence in the business of writing. She lives in Ohio with her husband, the infamous Mr. Rylon, and their cat, Frodo. When she can escape her purple office, she loves to travel the world, avoid speeding tickets in her beloved Sky, SCUBA dive, hunt Pokemon, and–of course–read.

Jayne Loves To Hear From Readers
www.jaynerylon.com
contact@jaynerylon.com
PO Box 10, Pickerington, OH 43147

ALSO BY JAYNE RYLON

4-EVER

A New Adult Reverse Harem Series

4-Ever Theirs

4-Ever Mine

EVER AFTER DUET

Reverse Harem Featuring Characters From The 4-Ever Series

Fourplay

Fourkeeps

EVER & ALWAYS DUET

Reverse Harem Featuring Characters from the 4-Ever and Ever After Duets

Four Money

Four Love

POWERTOOLS: THE ORIGINAL CREW

Five Guys Who Get It On With Each Other & One Girl. Enough Said?

Kate's Crew

Morgan's Surprise

Kayla's Gift

Devon's Pair

Nailed to the Wall

Hammer it Home

More the Merrier *NEW*

POWERTOOLS: HOT RODS

Powertools Spin Off. Keep up with the Crew plus...

Seven Guys & One Girl. Enough Said?

King Cobra

Mustang Sally

Super Nova

Rebel on the Run

Swinger Style

Barracuda's Heart

Touch of Amber

Long Time Coming

POWERTOOLS: HOT RIDES

Powertools and Hot Rods Spin Off.

Menage and Motorcycles

Wild Ride

Slow Ride

Hard Ride

Joy Ride

Rough Ride

POWERTOOLS: RETURN OF THE CREW

The original crew is back with more steamy menage stories!

Screwed

Drilled

Grind

Pound

MEN IN BLUE

Hot Cops Save Women In Danger

Night is Darkest

Razor's Edge

Mistress's Master

Spread Your Wings

Wounded Hearts

Bound For You

DIVEMASTERS

Sexy SCUBA Instructors By Day, Doms On A Mega-Yacht By Night

Going Down

Going Deep

Going Hard

STANDALONE

Menage

Middleman

Nice & Naughty

Contemporary

Where There's Smoke

Report For Booty

COMPASS BROTHERS

Modern Western Family Drama Plus Lots Of Steamy Sex

Northern Exposure

Southern Comfort

Eastern Ambitions

Western Ties

COMPASS GIRLS

Daughters Of The Compass Brothers Drive Their Dads Crazy And Fall In Love

Winter's Thaw

Hope Springs

Summer Fling

Falling Softly

COMPASS BOYS

Sons Of The Compass Brothers Fall In Love

Heaven on Earth

Into the Fire

Still Waters

Light as Air

PLAY DOCTOR

Naughty Sexual Psychology Experiments Anyone?

Dream Machine

Healing Touch

RED LIGHT

A Hooker Who Loves Her Job

Complete Red Light Series Boxset

FREE - Through My Window - FREE

Star

Can't Buy Love

Free For All

PICK YOUR PLEASURES
Choose Your Own Adventure Romances!
Pick Your Pleasure
Pick Your Pleasure 2

RACING FOR LOVE
MMF Menages With Race-Car Driver Heroes
Complete Series Boxset
Driven
Shifting Gears

PARANORMALS
Vampires, Witches, And A Man Trapped In A Painting
Paranormal Double Pack Boxset
Picture Perfect
Reborn

PENTHOUSE PLEASURES
Naughty Manhattanite Neighbors Find Kinky Love
Taboo
Kinky
Sinner
Mentor

ROAMING WITH THE RYLONS
Non-fiction Travelogues about Jayne & Mr. Rylon's Adventures
Australia and New Zealand

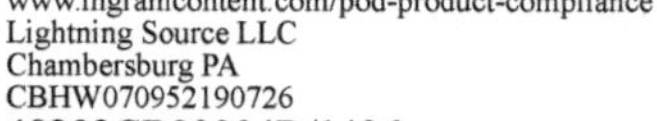